# RELUCTANT INFORMER

## WAR GIRL SERIES, BOOK 4

## MARION KUMMEROW

**Reluctant Informer** - War Girl Series, Book 4

Marion Kummerow

ISBN Paperback 978-3-948865-12-2

Cover Design by http://www.StunningBookCovers.com

Cover Photo: Bundesarchiv, Bild 102-16180 / CC-BY-SA 3.0

https://creativecommons.org/licenses/by-sa/3.0/de/deed.en

# CONTENTS

# READER GROUP

## Marion's Reader Group

Sign up for my reader group to receive exclusive background information and be the first one to know when a new book is released.

http://kummerow.info/subscribe

# INTRODUCTION

**When the Gestapo extends an** *offer,* **there's no way to refuse.**

Sabine Mahler never imagined going against the sinister Gestapo, until they made her an offer she couldn't refuse. With her husband in their hands, his life depends on her willingness to cooperate.

Will she be able to save her husband and the resistance organization she's tasked to take out?

# CHAPTER 1

*Berlin, February 1944*

Sabine and her husband of five years Werner sat at their kitchen table having dinner. On the radio, Goebbels's propaganda ministry raved on about yet another glorious victory of the Reich. She wondered whether anyone still believed those lies.

But she didn't voice her concerns. Not because their small row house on the outskirts of Berlin had paper-thin walls and the sounds of their neighbors on either side could easily be heard. No, she had made it a habit to mind her own business and not complain.

What difference would it make anyway?

Food rationing. Lack of adequate transportation. The horrid nightly bombings by the Allies. The god-awful work in the munitions factory. There was nothing she could do about any of it.

She didn't even complain, the way some of her work

colleagues did, about the ever-increasing quotas they had to fill. The soldiers needed rifles, and complaining about exhausted feet and numb hands would only bring the wrath of her superior upon her. It wouldn't change a thing in the greater scheme of warfare.

Weapons were needed and someone had to make them. People who stuck their noses into someone else's business tended to disappear. That wouldn't happen to her.

"How was your day?" Sabine gave Werner a tired smile as the news report ended. Usually he would pull her onto his lap after finishing dinner, but not today. He hadn't even bothered to change out of his uniform, and merely unbuttoned the top two buttons on his shirt and rolled up his shirt sleeves.

Werner sighed and a look of sadness flashed over his face. "There was another incident with the SS." He paused for a long moment, reluctant to tell her what bothered him.

"What happened this time?" She knew how much he adored being a fireman. His father and grandfather both had been firemen, and it was only natural that he would follow in their footsteps. But the work had changed so much, it wore on his soul, until most of the joy drained away. Instead of serving and protecting his fellow citizens, he had to stand by helplessly and watch the atrocities the SS or Gestapo committed. He rarely complained, afraid to utter criticism against the Party, but she knew how much he hated the cruelty of the regime.

Sabine sat quietly, waiting for him to speak again. The pained expression on his face struck panic in her heart. It beat so fast, she thought it might gallop out of control. After a few minutes, he finally looked up, and she read the sorrow in his eyes.

"They torched another building. With people inside, women and children. Sabine, some of them were jumping from the windows in their desperation, and the SS men trampled on those who survived the fall. God, it seems wrong to even call those thugs men. What I saw today was devoid of any humanity or compassion..." He paused for a moment and she saw a depth of bleakness in his eyes she'd not seen before.

She reached across the table and gripped his hand. "You saw this?"

Werner hid his face between his palms. "Yes. A neighbor called us, but the SS wouldn't let us extinguish the fire, not until everyone inside was burned alive and the building in ruins." He looked at her, dampness shimmering in his eyes. "Slaughtered. Everyone. Even babies. For allegedly housing traitors."

"This is so awful." Sabine squeezed her husband's hand in sympathy.

"I wanted to do something, anything ...but what could I do?" He buried his head between his hands.

"Don't blame yourself. You couldn't have done a thing. You did right by staying out of it, or they might have killed you too."

Werner looked at her and his gaze turned to steel. "I've been staying out of it for such a long time and look what's happening. The SS has more power now than ever before. Maybe it's time we stopped minding our own business and stood up against injustice."

Sabine released his hand, her eyes going wide at his statement. "Werner, that's crazy talk. You don't mean that."

"I do mean it. Germany, the Germany I love, isn't a country of insane lunatics who bully others and kill anyone who has a different opinion..." He jumped up and paced the kitchen.

"Shush! Or the neighbors might hear!" Sabine pushed up from her chair and stepped into his path.

"See where this has got us?" He lowered his voice to a whisper. "I can't even tell my wife how sick and tired I am of these thugs. And thugs they are, make no mistake."

Sabine agreed with her husband on the thug part, but getting involved would put their safety at risk. Those people must have done something illegal. Why else would the SS go after them? "Don't talk like that. Promise me you won't do anything stupid. Simply do your job and ignore what's happening around you. Please!"

Werner took hold of her hips and moved her out of his way to take up his pacing again. "Ignore it? How can I ignore German women and children being slaughtered like this? My job is to protect..."

"And you're doing just that, but the Nazis have changed the ways things are done. You should be grateful that your job as fireman exempts you from serving at the front."

Werner turned around and stepped in front of her, his handsome face mere inches away. He glanced down at her for a long moment and then sighed loudly. "I know, and I'm grateful, but...this is not right...we should...put out fires, not watch toddlers and their mothers perish..."

"You have to distance yourself from what happened today. You can't draw attention to yourself or let anyone suspect that you object to their methods. That would be painting a target on your back – and mine." She wrapped her arms around his chest, hoping her pleading words would ring true with him. They had endured so much together.

"I know. I just needed to vent my emotions for a few moments." He hugged her, resting his chin on the top of her head.

Sabine pushed back a bit and looked him in the eyes. "Promise me you won't do anything stupid? I love you so much; I couldn't live without you."

"I promise." Finally, his usual smile returned as he gathered her into his arms and carried her to their bed. "I love you too, Sabine. I'd do anything for you."

# CHAPTER 2

Sabine stared across the expanse of the factory, trying to convince herself that this job wasn't so bad. Unfortunately, her mind didn't buy it and dissatisfaction seeped into her soul like bitter medicine. In fact, she hated working at the factory, but then again, she recognized the futility of any form of protest.

The *Arbeitsamt* had assigned her to work there and like any good citizen, she'd obeyed. While her current station was monotonous, the work was easy and not physically demanding. As far as jobs went, there were much worse positions out there and she had no desire to experience any of them personally. Like cleaning the rubble from the streets after the air raids. Although, to tell the truth, she suspected such hard labor served as some kind of penal assignment. The people doing it looked awfully like prisoners in their striped uniforms.

She side-glanced at the empty station right next to her. The woman working that station hadn't shown up for work two days ago and no one seemed to know her whereabouts. Sabine wondered whether she'd been killed during a bombing or maybe taken away by the Gestapo. Those things happened, although they obviously were seldom confirmed.

Her hands busy assembling rifle parts, she noticed one of the supervisors heading in her direction and ducked her head, keeping her eyes focused on the task. She'd made it a habit to make herself as invisible as possible, and rarely socialized with her coworkers.

Women who irritated the supervisors never fared well. They usually got moved to stations with a higher risk of injury or physically hard work.

"Frau Mahler," her superior's voice interrupted her musings.

"Yes?" She looked up at the old and well-fed man.

"This is your new coworker, Frau Klausen. I want you to show her the ropes." He stepped aside to give way to an older woman standing behind him. Frau Klausen had graying hair, and the wrinkles lining her face testified as much to her age as to the privations every Berlin woman had to suffer on a daily basis. The somber black dress that peeked out from under the ugly grey-blue protective apron spoke of the hardships of more than five years of war and clothing rationing.

"Of course, Herr Meier." Sabine groaned inwardly. Teaching Frau Klausen the ropes would set her back in reaching her own quota, which was never a good thing.

Herr Meier disappeared, leaving a shell-shocked-looking Frau Klausen standing next to Sabine. Sabine couldn't help but feel sympathy for the older woman.

"Thank you for teaching me, Frau Mahler," Frau Klausen

said. "This is the first time in my life I'm required to work outside the house, but I promise I'm a quick study."

Sabine nodded, but then thought better of it and gave her a smile. "You'll get the hang of it pretty soon. Here, I'll show you." She proceeded to show her new coworker the motions needed to assemble the standard-issue Karabiner 98k.

Frau Klausen looked even more shell-shocked when she noticed what emerged from under Sabine's hands. As promised, Frau Klausen was a quick study and didn't need much handholding. Sabine especially appreciated her quietude. The older woman didn't chat on incessantly about fashion, gossip or men like some of her younger coworkers did.

Throughout the morning Sabine kept an eye on her coworker, giving her tips on how to work faster or with more accuracy. But apart from this, she kept her distance, as there was no reason to become friendly with anyone.

As the gong sounded to indicate lunch break, Sabine rubbed her hands across the rough material of the protective apron. She set the rifle parts down to walk to the small rest area, where she'd earlier stored her lunch. She'd already taken a few steps away from her workstation when she looked back to see a completely out-of-her-depth Frau Klausen.

"Did they give you a tour of the factory yet?" she asked.

"Not yet. I suppose I'll have to figure things out on my own," Frau Klausen said with a tired smile, rubbing her back and stretching her shoulders.

Sabine sighed. "Come with me. I'll show you where everything is."

"Thank you. That is very kind of you. Have you worked here for long?" Frau Klausen asked, falling into step beside her.

Sabine shrugged her shoulders. "Long enough to know this is not my dream job, but it helps the war effort so…here I am." They arrived at the break room where the women had the opportunity to heat up their lunch or buy something with their ration cards. Most of them, though, just ate some lukewarm soup brought in a thermos, or a hearty sandwich.

Another coworker, Elise, approached them. Sabine involuntarily ducked her head, because she feared the inevitable.

"Hi, I'm Elise. What's your name?"

"Frau Klausen." The older woman seemed as unwilling to engage in random chit-chat as Sabine herself.

"How come an old lady like you works here?" Elise asked, and Sabine inwardly cringed.

But Frau Klausen took it in stride and answered with a pleasant voice, "My husband is a prisoner of war in Russia and our four kids are all grown and don't need me anymore, so the *Arbeitsamt* decided I could best serve the Fatherland working here."

"Oh yes, isn't it exciting?" Elise jumped up and down, clapping her hands. "We're helping the Führer to win the war. Assembling rifles. That's such an important job to do for a young girl like me, don't you think?"

"Your enthusiasm is admirable," Frau Klausen said with a voice entirely devoid of the enthusiasm she'd just praised.

"Yes. Obviously, I would have loved to work for the Propaganda Ministry, typing up all those wonderful speeches Goebbels and his employees are giving. But my typing speed was too slow…and you know, I never was really keen on school. I always thought I'd marry by eighteen and have a handful of children…but my sweetheart left for war, and so here I am doing my bit. It's such important work. Can you even imagine, that one of the rifles I assembled may be given to a brave German soldier to kill those depraved Russians?" Elise's face brightened the room like anti-aircraft searchlights at night.

Frau Klausen's lips pursed at the gush of words from the young woman and she bit into a piece of bread with heavenly-smelling cheese.

"So, what are your children doing?" Elise asked.

"My only son is a Wehrmacht soldier, currently somewhere in occupied Poland. He might be carrying one of your rifles—"

"Oh yes, isn't that exciting?" Elise blurted out and started another monologue about the greatness of war in general, and Hitler in particular. Sabine had long ago decided to tune out the exuberance from Elise and some of the other girls. She might have been like them five years ago, but ever since she'd had two miscarriages she valued life a lot more. And war meant taking lives. Her stomach clenched. Two years had passed since the last miscarriage, and she still threatened to break out in tears every time she saw a pregnant woman.

Thankfully, the bell announcing the end of lunch break tore her from her morose thoughts.

"Lunchtime is over," Sabine said, standing up and smoothing her hands over her hair, to make sure the rolls and curls were still in place. At work they weren't allowed to wear their hair down due to the risk of injury, so she'd ingeniously invented a special hairdo that had all the elegance of the hair down, combined with the required work safety rules. She secretly called it the *Sabine Roll*.

"Thank you for showing me around and eating lunch with me," Frau Klausen said on the way back to their workstations.

"You're very welcome." Sabine increased her work pace to make up for the time lost demonstrating Frau Klausen the tasks, and spent the remainder of her shift thinking about her new coworker.

It was obvious that the woman missed her husband and son very much. Although she hadn't exactly said so, the longing on her face had given her away. Sabine knew she herself was privileged, because Werner's work made him exempt from service, and she could only wonder how she would cope should he be sent away.

She loved him so much that just imagining something happening to him tore at her heart. Even after five years of marriage she felt the same butterflies and wobbly knees as on the day he first kissed her. A smile escaped her expression of concentration. Tragedies like the loss of their unborn babies could tear a couple apart or bond them tighter together. In her case the latter was true.

# CHAPTER 3

"Sabine," a voice called to her as she stepped out of the small row house where she and Werner lived.

She turned toward the voice to see Lily Kerber, her neighbor and former classmate, waving to her from the door of her own home. Lily had lived alone since her mother died a couple of years ago. Sabine always wondered how Lily managed to keep the house for herself, when so many others were assigned bombed-out victims to live with them.

"Good morning, Lily. How are you?"

"Fine, thanks. I saw Werner come home a while ago. Is he working nights again?"

"Yes. He'll sleep most of the day now and will be leaving again when I return from work." Sabine and Lily exchanged small talk every now and then, the way neighbors did, but they had never been close friends, despite the fact that they'd grown up on the same street and attended the same class at school.

Lily had been the popular girl at school, the one all the boys courted: the first one to show female curves, and the only one to have the audacity to smoke in public.

"That must be so hard for you." Lily pouted her carefully painted lips. "Would you like to join me in going out to dinner this week?"

Sabine raised a brow. After knowing Lily for almost twenty years, this was the first time she'd ever invited her out. "Uhm, well…Werner's schedule is all over the place and I have to work…"

"You said he's working night shifts, so what would stop two lonely women from keeping each other company? How about tomorrow night?"

Sabine almost fell backwards. Lily had never been lonely in her life. Even in middle school Sabine had lost count of the many admirers in Lily's life, and that number hadn't changed since. Sabine didn't want to assume anything improper, since Lily never invited any of the men inside, but she sure knew how to turn heads.

For lack of a valid reason to deny the request, Sabine said, "Thank you. I'd love to meet up and chat about old times."

"Good, I'll ring at seven p.m. My treat." Lily said with a broad smile and waved a gloved hand, before she stepped back inside her house, and shut the door.

Sabine looked after her for a long moment, muttering beneath her breath, "Strange. That was just strange."

Shaking off her concern, she walked to the bus stop and waited for the line taking her to work. In the evening, she arrived home just as Werner pulled on his uniform for the upcoming night shift.

Lily and her invitation had been uppermost in Sabine's mind most of the day. Now that she thought about it, her neighbor seemed to be untouched by the hardships of war everyone else had to cope with. Today, she'd worn a flashy red woolen coat that must have cost a year's supply of ration cards. And in contrast to Sabine's own shabby coat, it didn't hang loose on her curvy frame.

Sabine had lost at least ten pounds over the years and sometimes Werner joked that her protruding ribs would give him bruises. What wouldn't she give for a dozen pounds more on her scrawny bones? But then, nobody in Berlin had fat on their hips anymore.

"Darling, I'm home." She walked over to wrap her arms around Werner and stood on her tiptoes to receive his kiss.

"I wish I could stay," he said. "But on the weekend, I'll be off duty and I thought we could go to the Wannsee lake. See whether it's still frozen? Take a walk across the ice?"

"That would be nice." Sabine grabbed his neck to press another kiss on his lips. There were so few fun things to do these days, a trip to the lake – even in wintertime – seemed like paradise. Then she remembered the dinner invitation and said, "Lily invited me to join her for dinner tomorrow."

Werner looked up, confusion on his face. "Lily Kerber? Our neighbor?"

"Yes, her. She asked me this morning and even offered to pay. I don't quite know what to make of her invitation."

"Maybe she's just trying to be your friend?" he said, moving out of Sabine's embrace to finish dressing.

"After ignoring me for twenty years? I don't know." Sabine paused, unsure whether she should voice her suspicions. She usually didn't spread gossip, but if she were to have dinner with Lily, Werner needed to know. It wouldn't be appropriate if the wife of a fireman were seen with a woman of dubious reputation. "Have you noticed that she doesn't seem to be...hard-pressed... like everyone else?"

"In what way?" Werner put the cap on his short brown hair, and the breath caught in her breast at his dashing looks.

"Well, she's always wearing new clothes. Things the rest of us stopped even dreaming about long ago. And eating out and offering to pay for me as well...that just seems odd."

Werner poked her nose. "You worry too much, *Schätzchen*. Lily probably has fetched herself a lover high up. An influential Party member would be able to afford giving her all those clothes you seem to yearn for...although I do like you a lot without clothes."

Sabine's face heated up to the roots of her hair. "That's not very moral..."

"I can't find anything immoral about enjoying my wife," Werner teased her, and she felt the heated blush intensifying. It wasn't that she didn't enjoy her marital obligations, but why did he have to talk about it?

"I didn't mean us...I meant Lily, if that's even what she's doing..." Sabine covered her mouth with her hand, averting her eyes from her husband.

"Times have changed. Those things happen." Werner laughed at her. "People don't necessarily marry anymore to share a bed, you know?"

"I know that," Sabine said, giving him another hug and lingering long enough to let herself be reminded how safe she always felt in his arms. He was her protector, the strong man who always looked out for her. And if they hadn't been so unfortunate as to lose two babies, she'd be happily at home tending to her small family instead of having to work in that awful factory producing weapons.

"Well, then. Enjoy a lovely dinner with Lily and don't worry so much. How the money came her way is none of your concern." He pressed a kiss on her lips, before he walked out the door. "I'll see you in the morning, *Schätzchen.*"

Sabine busied herself doing the chores around the house. Cleaning, dusting, washing. And preparing a meal for Werner when he came home in the morning after a long night shift.

Then she retreated to bed, trying not to worry about the unusual invitation her neighbor had extended. Probably Lily was simply as lonely as Sabine was and needed some company.

# CHAPTER 4

The next day Lily knocked on the door as soon as Sabine returned from work.

"I just came home," she said and invited her neighbor inside. As always Lily looked the part of a frivolous actress with her red coat and a fashionable hat in the same color, but it was when she took it off to hang it on the coat rack that Sabine's breath hitched. Lily wore a shimmering silk dress in beige and copper tones that matched the copper color of her hair. The dress was molded to her body, exposing perfectly rounded breasts and hips – a luxury not many women possessed after years of rationing.

"You look beautiful," Sabine complimented her neighbor and added, "Make yourself at home, while I get changed."

"Take your time," Lily said, inspecting Sabine's home. All the houses on the street featured the same shape: a kitchen and a small sitting room on the ground floor and two tiny bedrooms and a bathroom upstairs. But the pride of the owners were the modern water toilets just beside the main entrance, which meant they didn't have to trudge to the outhouse anymore or use a chamber pot at night.

Sabine disappeared upstairs and dressed in her nicest outfit, a dark blue two-piece suit with a material-saving pencil skirt, even knowing she could never compete with Lily. A silk dress!

When she returned downstairs, Lily was looking at the photographs from Werner and Sabine's wedding and asked, "Werner is a very handsome man. How's he doing?"

"He loves being a fireman, but…" Sabine caught herself just in time before she said anything compromising. It was no one's business that Werner disliked the way the SS interfered with his work. "…the weeks with the night shifts are hard."

"I can only imagine! Although I admire him for becoming a fireman. We need strong and dedicated men to protect us." Lily put the framed photograph back on the chest of drawers.

Sabine looked at the picture of herself and Werner on their wedding day and as always, the butterflies started up in her stomach.

"You do love him, don't you?" Lily asked with a soft voice.

Surprised at her neighbor's sudden perception, Sabine said, "Yes. He's the best thing that ever happened to me. I couldn't imagine having to live without him."

"The two of you are a great pair. Shall we go?"

"Sure." Sabine followed Lily to the nearest bus stop. "Where are we going?"

"It's a surprise, but I'm sure you'll love it." Lily giggled.

For lack of anything better to say, Sabine engaged Lily in

the safest topic of them all: the weather. As a child, it had always struck her as peculiar how adults could literally talk for half an hour about the current, future or past weather. And now she resorted to the same tactic when she didn't know what else to say and couldn't let the conversation descend into uncomfortable silence.

The bus arrived and, despite its being crowded with passengers, it took Lily only one of her dashing smiles to make an elderly man offer her his place. Sabine secretly rolled her eyes. Nobody ever did this for her. What was it about her neighbor that all the men seemed to dance to her tune?

"We have to get off at the next stop," Lily said.

Once off the bus, Sabine looked around the affluent neighborhood. "Where are we?"

"Charlottenburg, home of one of the best restaurants in Berlin." Lily tugged at her gloves and interlaced arms with Sabine.

Lily's bizarre behavior hit Sabine in the middle of her chest with a stab of discomfort. In twenty years of knowing each other, Lily had never graced Sabine with any kind of interest. She lifted her face up into the dark sky, trying to get past the queasy feeling in her stomach.

"You're still working at the gun factory?" Lily asked as they turned around the corner.

"Yes. It's been very busy recently." Sabine sighed, not wishing to go into detail about her tedious work.

"It doesn't sound like you enjoy the work," Lily said.

"It's important for the war effort, so I don't complain, but I could think of more pleasant things to do with my time."

Lily stopped in her tracks and stared at Sabine, breaking out into laughter. "Who wouldn't? I couldn't imagine slaving away day in day out in a factory like you do."

Sabine's eyes widened.

"There are definitely easier ways to help the war effort. I see we are on the same page," Lily said, taking up her pace again. "We're almost there."

Several minutes later, they reached their destination. The liveried employee at the entrance greeted them, "Welcome, ladies, do you have a reservation?"

"A table for two. Kerber is the name," Lily answered gracefully and cast a charming smile at the poor employee, who didn't know what hit him. Blissfully ignoring Sabine, he almost fell over backwards to lead Lily inside and help her out of her fancy coat.

Sabine studied the menu in disbelief. Things she'd long forgotten that existed graced the menu. Lamb. Salmon. Oranges. Real coffee. Her mouth watered just looking at the words.

After they ordered their meals, Lily retrieved an elegant, black cigarette holder from her purse and moments later the waiter dashed to their table to light the cigarette for her. Inhaling deeply, she leaned back and then puffed out little smoke clouds with a satisfied smile.

"There's nothing more relaxing than a good gasper," Lily said, before she squinted her eyes for a moment in a pensive expression. "Would you like one?"

"No, thanks, I don't smoke," Sabine said. Besides the fact that cigarettes were expensive, and the rations could better be used for food, Sabine had never approved of women smoking. It was frivolous.

Lily nodded and then abruptly changed the topic. "I understand an older woman came to work at the munition factory a few weeks ago. A Frau Klausen?"

Sabine looked at her, confused at the direction the conversation had taken. "Yes. Do you know her?"

"She's quite a bit older than the other workers. Does she appear to be getting along alright?" Lily asked, ignoring Sabine's question.

"I guess so." Sabine had come to like her new coworker, because she was quiet and never asked nosy questions or tried to pry private details from anyone. In fact, Frau Klausen never talked about any other topic than her children when they were still young – or the weather.

"But she works next to you, correct?" Lily asked, leaning back and taking another drag on her cigarette.

"Yes, she does." Sabine paused, not sure what to make of this interrogation. She hated giving away personal details and tried to mind only her own business. "Why are you asking about her? Do you know her?"

"Not personally." Lily looked around and then leaned forward, lowering her voice slightly. "I'm working for the government and Frau Klausen's name appeared on a watch list as a potential enemy of the Reich."

"What?" Sabine gasped, swiftly putting a hand in front of her mouth. That accusation was completely unbelievable. Or maybe it wasn't. Even if it was, Sabine didn't care either way. That was none of her business.

"I'm afraid so, yes." Lily observed Sabine behind heavy eyelashes, painted in perfect black with mascara. "Would you be willing to relay information on Frau Klausen to me?"

"Me? Information about Frau Klausen? To you?" Sabine

felt like a complete idiot repeating Lily's request. "No. I'd rather mind my own business."

Lily frowned at her, giving her a harsh look and an even sterner verbal warning. "That is no way to stay alive during these treacherous times. The only way to keep yourself safe is to join the winning party. That's what I've done and it's an opportunity I'm offering to you. Either you're for the government or you're against it. There is no middle ground."

Sabine's head spun as Lily stopped speaking long enough for the waiter to serve their food. Lily graced him with a measured smile and he wandered off again, grinning like a schoolboy. Lily had always had the ability to make men melt into puddles at her feet.

For many years Sabine had been jealous, until she fell in love with Werner, two years senior, attending the same school. The one man – boy back then – who'd never succumbed to Lily's charms. Not that she hadn't tried.

Lily cleared her throat and Sabine stopped her musings. "My sponsors aren't stingy. They reward those who work for them generously. All this," she pointed at the table with its exquisite-smelling meals, "wouldn't be possible without their generosity." Then Lily cut her salmon and pierced a small piece with her fork, before she dipped it into honey mustard sauce.

Sabine followed suit, her mouth watering even before she put a piece of duck with orange-chestnut filling into it. The sweet-sour taste slid across her tongue, as she carefully chewed the fatty meat.

For a while Lily seemed content to talk about food in all forms, shapes and tastes. As they finished their meal, the waiter brought real coffee and even a dark chocolate praline.

"So, have you thought about my offer? It's not hard work and the Führer will reward you for it," Lily said, sipping at her coffee while holding the cigarette holder in her other hand. She could have stepped right out of a motion picture.

"What exactly do you do?" Sabine couldn't help but ask.

Lily leaned forward and whispered, "Well, I gather delicate information. My sponsors see that I am invited to the right kind of parties and events, where I meet the suspect, usually a rich and powerful man, to find out where his allegiance lies."

"And they tell you just like that?"

"Of course not, silly," Lily broke out into sparkling laughter, drawing all eyes to them. She lowered her voice to a whisper again. "A bit more effort is needed to make the target open up. You wouldn't believe the amount of information a man gives you, when he finds you *willing*."

Sabine felt herself blush all the way down to her toes. She must have misunderstood. But the way Lily pursed her lips, to give an air-kiss, didn't leave much room for misinterpretation.

"I'm a married woman! I couldn't do that," Sabine protested in shock.

Lily only grinned at her. "You'd be surprised what you could do given the proper motivation. Besides, there are other ways to get information."

"What exactly would I have to do?" Sabine asked, dreading the answer.

"Not much. Just telling me what Frau Klausen says and

does. Whom she's friendly with, what she does in her leisure time."

"I'm not really talking to her except about the weather and her children," Sabine twisted her hands fretfully in her lap, while she stared at the far wall, wishing to return home and lock herself into her bedroom until Werner came home in the morning.

Lily cocked her head to the side and suggested, "Why don't you sleep on my offer and then get back to me with your answer? The government is very generous to those who help them."

Sabine nodded, not knowing what else to do. If the offer was so generous, then why did she feel like a mouse caught in a trap?

# CHAPTER 5

S abine slept fitfully all night, plagued with nightmares about dark-clothed men coming after her and asking for Frau Klausen. In the morning she woke with a shock to find a big man standing in front of her bed on this sunny Sunday morning.

Her heart racing, it took her almost a minute until she shook off the remains of her dream and recognized Werner, who'd just returned from his night shift.

"Sabine? What's wrong? Are you ill?" He sat down beside her, frowning when he clasped her cold hands. He pulled them between his own and started rubbing them. "Sabine. Talk to me, please! You were screaming in your sleep."

She shook her head and gave the shadow of a smile. "It's nothing; I just had a bad dream."

"A bad dream? That's all it was?" He slipped beneath the covers at her side and wrapped his arms around her. "You're still shivering."

She couldn't deny the truth of his words as she struggled

to draw breath. Too strong were the images of the dark-clad men…Since Werner wouldn't give up until he'd coaxed the truth out of her, she decided to let the cat out of the bag. "Lily asked me to spy on a coworker who supposedly is an enemy of the Reich."

Werner drew in a breath and she felt his heartbeat speeding up. "She wants you to spy for the Gestapo?"

"She never mentioned the Gestapo by name, but I guess so. She said I would be generously rewarded for relaying information and would do my country a great service." Sabine turned in his arms to look into his eyes. "Werner, I'm scared. I don't want to get involved with these people."

He squeezed her hands and nodded, his voice serene. "Just as well. SD, SS, or Gestapo – one agency is worse than the next. It's best to stay as far away from them as possible."

She knew he talked from experience. In his work as a fireman he was often forced to work closely together with those agencies and he rarely found a nice word to say about any of them.

"What did you tell her?" he asked after a long silence.

"That I would think about it," Sabine said, leaning against his warm chest. In his arms she felt safe, in his arms she'd even confront the Gestapo.

"That's good. Continue to let her believe you are considering her proposal. Stall for more time. In fact, we should think about leaving the country."

Sabine groaned. "That's a little drastic, don't you think? Nobody's going to do me any harm, just because I refuse to become a spy. I haven't done anything wrong. Neither have you. We're both law-abiding citizens, we have nothing to fear."

Werner looked at her with fear in his beautiful blue-grey eyes. "Things have changed. They're not what they used to be."

"You think I'm wrong?"

"I think you're being naïve if you believe there is nothing to it. I've seen firsthand how these thugs operate."

Sabine rested her head on his chest once more, and Werner rubbed his hand up and down her back. She wore only her nightgown and when he slipped one hand beneath it, she forgot all about Lily's proposal and turned her head to give him access to her lips.

"I want you and since you don't have to leave for work, there's no need to rush," he murmured against the soft skin of her neck. Sabine purred her agreement and he divested her of the nightgown before he slipped out of his own clothes and made sweet love to her.

Several hours later, while Werner slept, she prepared a meal for them and took it upstairs on a tray to wake him up.

"I love you, *Schätzchen*," he said when he opened his eyes and then invited her to sit beside him and share the meal. "Promise me you'll be careful in dealing with Lily?"

# CHAPTER 6

Two days later Sabine's supervisor, Herr Meier, called for a meeting during lunch hour. Such meetings were never a source of good news, and the women entered the assembly place with long faces.

"Twenty-seven employees called in sick with the flu," Herr Meier said. Sabine groaned inwardly because she already knew what he would say next. "Our production is directly linked to the war effort and only with enough rifles can our soldiers succeed. Even though we are short-handed we must meet our daily quota. To remedy this situation, everyone will stay two hours longer today and come in one hour early tomorrow."

Nobody cheered. But nobody objected, or groaned either.

"Total War! *Sieg heil!*" he shouted, shooting his right arm up in the Hitler salute.

"*Sieg heil!*" the women shouted back.

Sabine drudged back to her workstation grumbling

beneath her breath, when Frau Klausen fell in pace beside her.

"There's no use frowning, now is there? It won't change a thing and we'll all get a little extra in our paychecks come the end of the week," Frau Klausen said, glancing at Sabine's frown-lined forehead.

"A ten-hour shift is grueling enough, now they make us work twelve? When will this ever stop?" Sabine said with a vigorous shake of her head, only to raise her hand to check up on her *Sabine rolls*.

"You look lovely," Frau Klausen complimented her, but even the friendly words couldn't cheer up Sabine. She kept growling about the awful work in the awful factory.

"Frau Mahler, would you like to talk about something that makes you happy?" Frau Klausen suggested with a bright smile, apparently fed up with hearing Sabine's complaints.

"Why don't you stay out of my life?" Sabine snapped back at her. Moments later, guilt swamped her for speaking such harsh words to the woman who'd only tried to be friendly. It wasn't Frau Klausen's fault that Lily wanted Sabine to spy on her. Or maybe it was? Why did the older woman have to get on the bad side of the government? And when she insisted on sticking out her neck, why did she have to come and work next to Sabine?

She gritted her teeth, counting the minutes until her shift would be over and she could go home and tell Lily that she wasn't the right person for this job. She just couldn't do it.

Her feet ached, and she rubbed her back every so often to alleviate the pain located just above her tailbone. Would this horrendous shift ever end? Working as fast as humanely possible without injuring herself, she finally reached her increased quota and slipped out of one shoe to wriggle her toes, before walking over to the supervisor's station to hand in her tracking sheet.

"Well done, Frau Mahler," he said, giving her an appreciative glance. "You're not only fast but accurate. Help your neighbor finish her batch and then everyone should be ready to go."

Sabine trudged back to her workstation, when Frau Klausen met her halfway with a tired smile saying, "All done. I believe Elise has two more to assemble and then we'll finally be done."

She nodded and sighed. If Elise would work more instead of talking a mile a minute, she'd have finished a long time ago. Minutes later, the gong sounded to announce they had reached their quota and could all go home.

*Thank God!*

Sabine rushed from the factory, her mood foul and her temper on a hair-trigger. To make things worse, a gusty wind whipped snowflakes into her face, making her hunch her shoulders and wrap her headscarf tighter around her neck and shoulders.

How she wished to be somewhere else. In Spain, for example. That country hadn't joined the war and according to newspaper articles, it never snowed over there. Nor did the people have to endure rations, *Ersatzkaffee*, and constant air raids.

Despite the ugly weather she made it home in record time, only to find Lily coming out of the door at the very moment Sabine passed by her house. Ducking her head, she made for her own front door, pretending not to notice the other woman. But Lily stepped out onto the street and blocked Sabine's path.

"Hello, Sabine. How was your day?"

Sabine stopped and looked up at Lily, clad in a flashy evening gown glittering in golden tones beneath a dark brown sable coat. The ensemble probably cost more than Werner earned in a year. The conceited woman brandished the long cigarette holder as if she were some famous actress right off the silver screen. "I've had a very long, very tiring day."

Lily shrugged her shoulders, taking a drag off the cigarette before blowing the smoke out and giving Sabine a look devoid of any sympathy. "You haven't given me an answer to what we discussed..."

"I just told you I'm tired. It's cold and I want to go inside." Sabine gestured toward the front door of her home for emphasis. "I don't want to stand outside in the dark talking to you."

"Which is the very reason why you need to come onboard with me. Don't you see it? You wouldn't be so tired. You wouldn't have to work such long hours at the factory. You might not have to work at the factory at all."

Sabine gave a harsh laugh. "But you want me to work at the factory so that I can spy on my unsuspecting coworkers. If I worked fewer hours or quit, that would be defeating the purpose. Wouldn't it?" Sabine couldn't keep the sarcasm out of her voice.

"Well, you'd have to get the information on Frau Klausen before they'd let you quit. But then...well, there are plenty of other places you could be useful for the Reich."

"Like you?" Sabine felt the frustration snake up her spine. She'd rather stop working at the damned factory sooner than later, but not when it involved shady work for Lily's secret employer.

"Yes. There are always—"

Sabine cut her off with a cutting motion of her hand. "Lily, I'm not a tart like you. I won't sell my body to get information for the Nazis so that they can twist it all around and ruin someone else's life."

The high-pitched gasp and the indignant expression on Lily's face promised retribution, but Sabine's empathy had long since evaporated. The entire dammed-up discontent of her grueling day burst out of her. "And, since you're so eager to hear my answer, here it is: No. I will not work as a spy. Never." She pushed her way past Lily, heated spots burning on her cheeks, and stormed into her home.

She slammed the door shut, threw the bolt, and leaned against the door, her breath coming in ragged spurts. Unshed tears stung her eyes and threatened to overflow. Werner found her like this a few minutes later.

"Sabine? What's happened?" he asked in the soft voice that would usually calm her down and give her reassurance. Not today.

She pushed off the door and shook her head, shedding her coat, headscarf, and gloves. Without speaking a further word, she headed for the kitchen and put the kettle on the stove.

Only then did she dare to look at him, a queasy feeling snaking into her soul. "I really blew it with Lily," she said and recounted her exact words to him.

Werner's face remained set in stone, a clear indication he

was more than a bit worried. When she finished her story, he said solemnly, "I agree. Calling the woman a tart was probably not your wisest course of action. Maybe you should go over and apologize to her? Blame it on the vile day you had at work?"

"No. No. She is a slut – or worse. I shouldn't have called her out on her immoral behavior, but I'm not apologizing to that woman."

He was quiet for a moment and then held out his hand to her. "I have an idea. Why don't you change into your housedress and I'll make tea for us? After dinner I'll rub your back until you forget all about the hard day? How does that sound?"

Sabine pulled the whistling kettle from the burner and gave Werner a soft smile. "You are so good to me, even when I don't deserve it. I'll think about apologizing."

Werner kissed her on the forehead and then shooed her toward the bedroom. "Go."

Sabine hugged him before she walked upstairs to change into her robe. A hot tea and an early night sounded like the perfect remedy for the awful day she'd had.

# CHAPTER 7

*Several days later*

Sabine arrived home from work, expecting to find Werner home, but the house was empty. Since he sometimes got delayed during a fire, she put his dinner into the oven to keep warm and ate alone.

She switched on the radio to her favorite music program, the *Wunschkonzert*, where listeners could phone the radio station and ask for a song to be played. A load of laundry to iron and fold by her side, she sang to the popular tunes and her mood improved.

About halfway in to the program the mother of a son missing in action asked for the song *Ich weiß es wird einmal ein Wunder geschehen* – "I Know One Day a Miracle Will Happen" by Zarah Leander.

*Couldn't we all use a miracle?* Sabine thought, suddenly swept up in nostalgia. She ironed Werner's uniform shirts and hung them neatly in the closet. After finishing the entire basket of laundry, it was past eleven p.m., but there was still no sign of Werner.

She decided to call the fire station and inquire about his unusual delay. "Hello, I'm Frau Mahler and I was wondering if you'd know where my husband Werner Mahler was?"

The voice on the other end of the line interrupted her: "He's not here."

"Would you know where he is? His shift ended five hours ago and he's still not home."

"Ma'am, I'm sorry but I don't have any information. All I know is that he's not on duty anymore. Goodnight."

Sabine stared at the phone, her worry increasing tenfold. "Werner, where are you?" she asked the empty room, doing her best to keep her tears from falling.

Past midnight, she went to bed, but sleep proved elusive as she jumped at every little noise, wishing and praying for her husband to walk through the front door. She must have fallen asleep at some time, because the alarm tore her out of her dreams. Only half-awake she rolled over to his side of the bed – empty. Her eyes popped open in shock and she scanned the room for any evidence of his presence. Nothing.

She rushed downstairs, but the house was empty. No hat and no coat, except hers, hung on the rack beside the front door. Her heart as icy as her naked feet on the cold linoleum floor, she dressed in a hurry, forgoing the usual artwork of putting her hair into rolls. Skipping breakfast, Sabine grabbed her purse to visit the fire station before reporting for work.

The receptionist cast her eyes downward, pretending to

be busy with something, the moment Sabine stepped in front of her desk.

"Good morning, Fräulein Schulz," Sabine said.

"How can I help you?" the woman answered, still not looking her in the eyes.

Sabine's stomach did a double dip. The few times she'd met Fräulein Schulz before, she'd always been helpful and friendly. Taking a deep breath, she asked, "My husband Werner Mahler didn't come home last night. Any chance you would know his whereabouts?"

"I'm sorry. He's not here," Fräulein Schulz said, ducking her head and intently studying her fingernails.

Sabine wanted to grab her by the throat and shake her until she said something. Anything. *What happened to my Werner? And why won't you tell me?* she wanted to scream.

A man waiting in the queue behind her said, "Lady, there's more of us waiting." She stepped aside, letting the next person bring forward their concern. With nothing else to do, she walked toward the exit, her shoulders hunched forward, until she saw a colleague of her husband. "Hello, Ernst."

He waved at her with a serious face and shook her hand, saying in a soft voice, "Don't ask questions. Let it go."

She gasped at his words, unable to respond to him.

"Save yourself and don't ever return here again," he whispered before he quickly left the room, leaving Sabine stupefied.

*Don't ask questions? Let it go? We're talking about my husband, not some random stranger!* Sabine feared her knees would give out, and she mustered the little energy she had left to straighten her back and walk out of that damned fire station as if nothing had happened, when indeed, her entire life was collapsing around her.

Werner had disappeared, and those people knew more than they let on. She loved him. How could she forget about him? Abandon him? He wouldn't abandon her. Tears of frustration filled her eyes.

Just as she walked down the stairs in front of the building, someone grabbed her elbow and propelled her onto the sidewalk.

"Don't talk yet," he whispered, keeping up a vigorous pace.

She glanced at the man walking beside her and recognized Werner's superior. Her pulse ratcheted up to a hammering staccato, but somehow she managed to keep her face straight and her mouth closed until they'd rounded the next corner into a small alleyway. "I don't understand what's going on."

The officer gave her a sympathetic look, saying, "The Gestapo came yesterday and took Werner away."

Sabine gasped and covered her mouth to hold back the cry that wanted to escape. Tears pooled in her eyes and she shook her head. "Why?"

"The why usually doesn't matter. I'm urging you not to do anything stupid. There's nothing you can do to help him, but you can save yourself. Consider leaving town for a while. Werner would want you to be fine...."

"I can't do that. There must be some mistake. Can't anyone talk to them?"

"No one is going to interfere with the Gestapo. Go to work and do everything as you normally would. Don't go asking questions." With that said, he stepped out of the alleyway and disappeared back inside the station.

Sabine waited a few minutes, trying to contain the anger building inside. How could they all stand by and look away? He'd worked with these very people for so many years, some he even called friends, and they were all willing to abandon him in a heartbeat?

She allowed her rage to fuel her walk as she headed off for the factory. Arriving at the gates, she glanced at her wristwatch. *Late again.* She had only four minutes to change and sneak into her workstation before her shift began.

In her hurry to arrive on time, she hadn't noticed the ominous man blocking the entrance to the factory until she almost bumped into him.

# CHAPTER 8

"I'm sorry. I didn't see you there," she said with an apologetic smile.

"Sabine Mahler?"

"Yes. Why?" Sabine answered, wariness in her gaze and tension filling her limbs.

The man pointed toward a black vehicle parked at the curb. "Gestapo. You must come with me."

Violent fear rushed through her body, making it impossible to follow his order. Out of habit, she raised a hand to control whether her elegant hairdo had become undone, even whilst her knees shook. Usually, large ring curls rolled back from her face, forming an elegance rivaling that shown by the actresses that graced the silver screen. A bevy of pin curls kept the rest of her hair secured at the base of her neck, adding to the sophistication of the hairstyle. The perfect rolls and pinup curls in her honey-blonde hair had become her one extravagance amidst the depression of living in war-torn Berlin.

But her hand found only a tight bun at the nape of her neck. She barely noticed it. None of her former preoccupations mattered right now. She'd discarded her own rules and poked her head into things that were better left alone. And now the spirits she'd conjured up by visiting the firestation wouldn't be banished again.

"Frau Mahler? You need an extra invitation?" the Gestapo officer said with a movement of his right hand to his hip.

"N…n…no. I'm coming." Sabine somehow managed to order her legs to move toward the black vehicle. No manual existed outlining how to behave when the Gestapo extended an *invitation* to follow them. But she assumed her best chance to stay in one piece was to cooperate fully with whatever this man wanted.

He opened the back door of the vehicle and commanded, "Get in."

Sabine climbed inside, fear grabbing at her heart when he followed and sat beside her.

"Headquarters," he told the driver and within seconds, the vehicle sped down the street. Bicycles swerved in haste when they heard the vehicle approaching them and Sabine imagined seeing the fear on the faces of passersby.

She inched as far away from the man sitting with her as the confinement of the backseat allowed. For a fleeting moment, she even considered jumping out of the moving automobile.

But that would defy the purpose. She'd visited the firestation not because she wanted to get involved in politics, but because her beloved husband had disappeared. She clasped her hands together in her lap in the vain effort to control the tremble in her limbs. Her breathing ragged, she started to count to fifty and then again.

The man at her side seemed to have noticed her distress, although he must have been used to causing anguish all round, and said, "My boss only wants to talk to you. For now."

Sabine swallowed. Hard. His soothing statement hadn't assured her one bit. On the contrary, it felt like a concealed threat. Going back to counting, her mind raced faster than the vehicle speeding down Berlin's ruined streets. She tried to convince herself that there was no reason to panic. Not yet, anyway.

Maybe the rumors weren't true? Maybe the Gestapo weren't the thugs everyone painted them as. Sabine almost choked at her musings.

The Gestapo instilled terror into every German citizen, and with good reason. Werner had recounted numerous horror stories about the atrocities they committed on innocent and unsuspecting people. And now her beloved husband was in the hands of these depraved monsters. She had to be strong.

For him.

She kept her hands tightly woven together as they drove through the city, but her entire body trembled, giving away the ferocity of her terror. The driver finally stopped and Sabine looked outside the window, straight at the huge grey building with the beautiful ornaments over the windows and the pompous entrance.

The exterior beauty of the building stood in stark

contrast to the terror it evoked in everyone who didn't work there. Prinz-Albrecht-Strasse 8. Gestapo headquarters. Sabine was too young to remember, but the magnificent building had been an arts and crafts school before 1933 – a use much more suitable to its splendor.

"Get out," the Gestapo officer said.

Her heart thumping against her chest, Sabine made an effort to leave the vehicle without stumbling from nerves. She managed to follow him with tiny steps, her head held high, a smile plastered on her face to try and fool any passersby that her arrival was nothing unusual and not a lamb's being led to the slaughter.

The huge wooden door opened and the magnificence of the entrance hall took her breath away. Under different circumstances she would have relished the shining beauty of the marbled floor, the high ceilings decorated with artful stucco and the broad wooden stairs, polished by decades of use.

Passing through long hallways with closed doors, the officer led her up several stairways into the attic. With each step Sabine's stomach tied into a tighter knot, until she struggled to draw breath. She raised her hand to touch her carefully done rolls, just to remind herself that she was still well and alive – for now. But she found only a messy bun, the embodiment of her current predicament.

The attic showed no trace of splendor or magnificence. It was a dimly illuminated place with closed metal doors and an eerie silence that seemed full of the shadows of tortured souls. Sabine didn't consider herself superstitious, but right there and then, she sensed the presence of angry energy.

Her hand fell from her head to her heart, as she heard a bone-chilling shriek coming from behind one of the doors. She'd rather not know the source of the agony and tightened her lips to mask her expression, while secretly cursing her foolishness in investigating her husband's disappearance.

The officer opened a door and shoved her inside a small room that held nothing more than a table and two chairs. A single bare lightbulb hung directly above her head, illuminating the windowless room with harsh and unforgiving light.

"Sit," he said and disappeared, locking the door after him.

Sabine felt an icy chill crawling up her spine as she took a seat and stared at the grey walls covered with stains. Bloodstains.

She checked her wristwatch. Her superior would be livid because she hadn't arrived for the shift. Should she tell this to the Gestapo? In case anyone ever arrived to talk to her.

After checking her watch about one hundred times, less than thirty minutes had passed. Her left leg did an annoying wriggling and she couldn't stop it. What was worse, her left eyelid started twitching, too. Two more minutes passed and no sound or person entered the room. Would they leave her to rot in here?

She already imagined how her parched corpse would be hauled outside a few days from now. Another minute passed. The waiting grated on her nerves, making her an anxious wreck. She resorted to counting again. Slow, measured breathing and counting. One – Two – Seven

hundred sixty-five – Four thousand two hundred eighty-
one –

The door opened with a creak and she jumped.

"Kriminalkommissar Becker. You wished to see me?"
The Gestapo officer offered a smile that did not reach his
cold grey eyes.

Sabine would have liked to scream at his brazenness, but
she returned the same fake smile and said, "Please, what is
this about?"

Becker took the opposite seat, placed his elbows on the
table and steepled his hands together beneath his chin. He
stared at her for a long moment, before he spoke.

"I am here to make you an offer."

"An…offer? I don't understand."

He smirked. "Oh, I think you do, but we will play this
game all the way out. We need your help in a delicate case."

"My help?" Sabine felt as if she was caught in a nightmare as Kriminalkommissar Becker's words registered.

"Yes. We need information. I believe your neighbor
Fräulein Kerber already discussed this topic with you."

Sabine felt herself flush under his cold stare, memories
of the unpleasant dispute with her former classmate Lily
Kerber flooding her brain. Werner had, as always, been
right. She shouldn't have called Lily a tart. Actually, that
woman was a million times worse than a tart, as no doubt,
*she* was responsible for both Werner and Sabine being in
Gestapo custody right now.

"She mentioned something about working for the
government," Sabine pressed out through clenched teeth.

"Fräulein Kerber is a good German citizen, and you
should follow her footsteps and work for us." He scruti-

nized her face, saying, "It shall not be to your disadvantage. The Party is generous to those who support her."

The heat on her face intensified as she remembered what kind of *work* Lily did for the Gestapo. "Sir, I…I am a married woman…"

He cast her an amused smile. "We can change this, if you insist."

Sabine's eyes went round and she violently shook her head. "No. No, please."

"Everything would have been so much easier if you had only agreed to Fräulein Kerber's proposal. But since you didn't we had no choice but to give you an incentive." The smile suddenly reached his eyes as if he truly enjoyed the situation.

"An incentive?"

"Yes. Your husband is with us and I am willing to exchange his life for your collaboration."

"You have my husband? Can I see him?" Sabine jumped from her seat, but fell back when she realized she was giving away how much Werner meant to her.

"I'm afraid not. You've done nothing to earn such a reward. Once you start bringing me the requested information I may reconsider." He looked at her with an expectant expression on his face.

"But how do I know he's still alive?" Sabine asked, despite tremors running through her entire body.

"You'll have to trust me on this, Frau Mahler. He is alive. For now. But his fate lies in your hands." For several long moments silence filled the room until he raised his voice again, "I need your answer. Now."

Sabine stared at him, half expecting him to hit her, but

he just gazed at her with that cruel smile, apparently truly enjoying the cat and mouse game. Soon enough, her fear won the internal war and she dropped her gaze. After taking several breaths, desperately attempting to gain a small measure of control over her emotions, she asked, "What do I have to do?"

A glimmer of victory entered Becker's eyes. "Good choice. As Fräulein Kerber already explained, we need you to infiltrate a particularly devious resistance group and report back to us with the names of those in charge. We will take over from there."

The tiniest part of her still hoped she was having a nightmare and would soon wake up, but this cruel sadist sitting across the table was as real as the muffled cries behind the steel doors.

For the past ten years she'd kept her head down and minded her own business, convinced that cautious behavior would keep her out of harm's way. And suddenly she'd been thrown into the middle of a conspiracy plot with the Gestapo, some devious resistance group and her former classmate as main players. For God's sake, she wasn't a spy. She was a housewife enlisted to help the war effort by working in a munitions factory.

"Fine. How do I make contact with these subversives? And won't they be suspicious of me?" she asked, still reeling from the shock.

"Fräulein Kerber was right, you are an intelligent woman," Becker said, jotting down some notes on a piece of paper. Sabine wasn't sure whether she should acknowledge his compliment or not. In fact, she wasn't sure about anything, except that she would do everything in her power to save her husband's life.

"You must become friendly with Frau Klausen. We believe she's a key part of this group."

Sabine gasped. "The sweet elderly lady? She's a subversive?"

"She may look sweet on the outside, but in reality she's a devious and mean-spirited woman conspiring against the regime," Kriminalkommissar Becker said. "What do you know about her?"

"Not much. She came to work at the factory a little while ago. She has the workstation next to mine and had difficulties adapting at first, because as a mother of four she's never had to work before…" Sabine cast him an accusatory glance, before she continued, "I gave her some tips and after the first week she caught up and now always meets her quota."

"It's an unfortunate, albeit temporary, setback that mothers have to work outside the home to further the war effort. But Frau Klausen's children are all grown up and at least one of her daughters is involved in the hideous conspiracy against the core beliefs of our nation."

Sabine wondered what atrocious deeds Frau Klausen had done. She couldn't fathom the kind woman doing anything to hurt someone. "If you know she's an insurgent, why don't you simply arrest her?"

Becker shot her a hard glance that made her shiver. "It seems you're not so intelligent after all. We don't care about Frau Klausen. She's a minnow. We want the leaders of this heinous organization. Understood?"

"Yes, Herr Kriminalkommissar," Sabine pressed out before her voice could abandon her.

"You will befriend Frau Klausen, earn her trust, and report back to Lily Kerber everything you find out. Every last detail could be important, no matter how small."

Reporting to Lily? Sabine sensed the disgust forming a big lump in her throat, but she nodded her agreement and then launched the question burning on her tongue, "And my husband? Will you return him once I have finished this... task?"

Becker cocked his head. "That's what I said. If you work well, you'll get him back safe and sound."

"I'll do anything you want. Please don't kill him," Sabine said, before she could temper her impassioned plea. But he probably already knew her feelings. The satisfied smile that pursed his lips gave him away. He walked to the door and then gestured for her to follow him.

"Where are we going?"

"I will take you back to your work, unless you would prefer to walk the five miles."

She didn't want to spend a single moment longer in his presence, but she also didn't want to walk the long way back. If he drove her to work, she'd at least be there for the second half of her shift. As she hurried behind him through the long hallways of Gestapo headquarters, she saw him greet several other men who seemed to work here.

"Any luck?" a dark-haired man asked.

Becker answered with a smile, "If you don't break them with fear or pain, love for a family member will always do the trick."

Sabine felt rage taking hold of her. For him, holding her husband hostage was nothing more than a part of his atrocious game. What kind of depraved monster was he?

It dawned on her that maybe Werner's tales had painted the Gestapo in too good a light. The icy hand of desperation clenched around her heart. Could she even believe a promise made by a Gestapo officer?

How on earth had her ordinary life become such a muddled mess?

# CHAPTER 9

"Frau Mahler!" a gruff voice called to her as she tried to slip unseen to her workstation.

She turned to see her supervisor, Herr Meier, standing two steps away like a towering dragon with his arms crossed over his chest. "Where have you been all morning?"

"I'm sorry, just when I arrived here for my shift this morning, a..." She stopped, deciding she shouldn't tell anyone the Gestapo had blackmailed her into working for them. Her mind raced and she hung on to the first plausible idea: "...a policeman arrived to tell me my husband had been involved in an accident. He urged me to come with him straight away. I apologize, but I was too shocked to even remember that I should have told you." It wasn't difficult to look concerned about her husband's condition. He was in Gestapo custody, after all.

Herr Meier stared her down for a moment and then seemed to deflate. "Is your husband well?"

"Considering the circumstances, yes. I'll do everything to help him recover," Sabine said, clasping her hands together.

"Good. If you ever need to leave again, tell me first. Our work here is very important for the war effort and must be a priority to us all. For today I will allow you to leave after filling half of your quota. But this is the first and only time, and only because your husband is a fireman."

"Thank you, Herr Meier." Sabine hurried to squeeze into her workstation and took up her tedious task of assembling rifles. For the first time since beginning work in the factory, she rejoiced that her job didn't require mental effort. It gave her time to think over her bleak situation.

But whichever way she considered it, there was no way out. Werner was in the hands of the Gestapo and she had to become their informer if she wished for him to survive. A lump formed in her throat threatening to choke her. Her situation was making her desolate.

Although, what harm would it do to exchange some friendly words with Frau Klausen, and report back on noncommittal small talk? With that idea in mind, she even mustered a small smile.

The rumble in her stomach indicated lunchtime, and she ventured a glance at the clock hanging on the wall above the supervisor's office. Two thirty p.m. Lunch break was long over. Another, stronger rumble reminded her that she'd skipped breakfast as well.

When finally, the gong sounded to indicate afternoon break, Sabine scurried to her locker, only to remember that in her hurry to visit the fire station this morning, she'd forgotten to pack lunch. Her stomach would have to continue rumbling until she returned home in the evening.

A dreadful thought. Returning home to an empty place. Knowing that Werner was somewhere in a prison cell in that awful building in Prinz-Albrecht-Strasse.

"I overheard your conversation with Herr Meier," Frau Klausen said with a warm smile. "If there's anything I can do, please let me know."

Sabine stared at her with barely concealed hate. *For starters you could turn yourself in to the Gestapo and tell them to let my husband go free.*

Frau Klausen, though, seemed to mistake hate for grief and put a hand on Sabine's arm saying, "I will pray for your husband."

"He's…alive," Sabine stammered, pondering whether she should tell the older woman the truth. But how would that help? Instead she resigned herself to her new role as Gestapo informer and mustered a smile. "Thank you. Your kindness means a lot to me. Maybe we can talk a bit after our shift?"

Frau Klausen nodded, but sent her a suspicious glance and avoided talking to Sabine for the rest of the afternoon. Obviously she'd picked up on Sabine's desperation to become friendly with her. Or she'd simply thought it strange that after being so standoffish the last few weeks, Sabine now wanted to be friendly all of a sudden – or she knew about the Gestapo…

Icy droplets trickled down her neck, causing her to hunch her shoulders. With nothing better to do, she fumbled for her perfect rolls and curls, trying to find some reassurance in the normality of her life. Her fingers crudely reminded her of the truly extraordinary situation, when they found only the bun made in a hurry this very morning.

Tears stung at her eyes, as the revelation hit. Her entire life was shattering around her.

It was only a stupid hairdo. But this hairdo had been her last shred of hanging onto a happier life before the war. Reality had caught up with her.

After her shift she returned home, to an empty house with the ghost of Werner present in every single detail. The knowledge that he was a prisoner of the Gestapo took an iron grip around her heart, sending pangs of pain throughout her body and barely allowing her to breathe.

She brewed a cup of tea and settled on the couch, a blanket wrapped around her shoulders. She sat motionless, staring at the wall with tears in her eyes until sleep finally overtook her, her dreams infested with horrid images of torture and pain. And Lily with a smile upon her face, her fancy clothes and furs telling the tale of her allegiance to the Reich. When Sabine begged her for help, Lily puffed on her cigarette in the long holder and laughed at her. "Bet you're wishing you hadn't called me a slut, now."

Sabine woke with a start and reached out to her side, only to become aware that she was still half-lying on the couch. She knew she should go upstairs, but she couldn't bear the thought of sleeping in the bed she'd shared with Werner, afraid she'd never see him again.

# CHAPTER 10

Continuing to go through the motions of normal life was taking a toll on Sabine. It had been several days since she'd been summoned by Kriminalkommissar Becker, but his cruel, unpitying stare still followed her wherever she went. She jumped at every noise, fearing it was him or his henchmen, coming for her again.

Becoming friendly with Frau Klausen proved harder than imagined. For one thing, Sabine wasn't a social butterfly and didn't have much experience warming up to people. That had always been Werner's job. And while Frau Klausen was kind and warm-hearted, she never once talked about anything personal, except for tales about her children from years ago.

The restraint in the older woman's behavior left Sabine wondering if they would ever become the sort of friends the Reich hoped for.

Sunday morning arrived, and Sabine used her only day off to clean the small house. She was mopping the kitchen floor when a sharp knock came on the front door. *Whoever can this be?* She put water bucket and mop aside and wiped her hands on her apron before she opened the door.

And wished she hadn't.

Kriminalkommissar Becker stood in front of her, wearing what seemed his best Sunday suit. He raised his hat and asked, "Don't you want to invite me in?"

"Of course, please step inside," she said with a trembling voice, racking her brain about what he might want. Wasn't she supposed to report back to Lily? Not that she had done it, but there hadn't been anything newsworthy to report either.

"I've been patiently waiting for news, but now my patience is coming to an end," he said, stretching out on Werner's place on the couch as if he owned it.

Sabine fought the lump closing her throat and said, "I've tried to become friendly with Frau Klausen, just as you told me to. But so far she hasn't said anything remotely compromising."

"We know she works for the enemies of the Reich." Herr Becker glanced around, stopping at the framed wedding photograph of Sabine and Werner. He walked across the room and took the picture into his hands. "Such a beautiful couple. It would be a shame if you had to put a mourning edge around it."

Sabine almost collapsed from a heart attack the moment the macabre words left his thin lips, but Becker ignored her predicament. "I believe you'll have to try a lot harder." His finger caressed Werner's face on the photograph.

"If…if you already know Frau Klausen is part of the resistance, why don't you just arrest her?" she stammered.

"I told you before, and I will tell you again, Frau Mahler." He put the framed image back onto the chest of drawers and walked over to stand in front of Sabine. His nearness sped up her heartbeat. "Frau Klausen is a minnow. We want the heads of the organization. And you will lead us to them." His finger caressed her cheek the same way it had caressed her husband's picture, and Becker muttered, "Such a lovely couple...a real shame."

The icy grip of terror squeezing the air from her lungs, Sabine barely managed to keep upright, saying, "But how?"

"You should be grateful to have me thinking for you," Becker said, giving her a very smug grin, "because I have the perfect plan. You are going to move in with Frau Klausen and her daughter Ursula."

"Me? I'm going to move in with them?" Sabine couldn't believe her own ears. This man couldn't be serious about her moving in with random strangers.

"Yes. We need to speed things up." He licked his lips, enjoying this brilliant idea of his.

"But...I have a home of my own. Why would I move in with someone else? That doesn't make sense. And why would Frau Klausen even agree to this?" Sabine voiced the myriad of questions running around in her head.

"See, this is where I come into the picture. We'll visit the office for housing assignments and tell them your house was bombed, and thanks to my connections you'll be immediately assigned new housing."

Sabine shivered at the evil plan. "But...it would be...next to impossible that they would assign me to Frau Klausen and not to someplace else."

"You leave that part to me. My people can make just about anything happen in this country."

She didn't have the slightest doubt that he spoke the truth. No agency in Germany had more power than the Gestapo. If Becker wanted her to live with the Klausens, it would be one of his easiest tasks to arrange.

"So, how do you like my fantastic plan?" he asked, genuine joy visible in his face.

How could this sadistic monster be so...narcissistic? Didn't he have a modicum of feeling for his fellow humans? Actually, she already knew the answer and said, "It's a devious plan. I would never have been able to come up with this." Then a doubt entered her mind and she spoke aloud, "What if anyone finds out my house didn't really get bombed?"

Becker tilted his head to the side, a flash of sorrow at the shortcoming in his plan crossing his face. But it took only a few moments before he smiled again. "You truly are intelligent. You'll be an asset to us. Trust me, nobody will find out. You have one hour to pack what you wish to keep."

"One hour?" Sabine repeated, like she was soft in the head, still trying to process everything he'd said.

"I would suggest you don't waste a minute of it. And now please excuse me, I have things to arrange." Becker walked to the door and let himself out. Sabine followed him as if in a trance and leaned her back against the locked door.

Taking in the familiar sights of her small home, a shudder ran through her body when the realization hit her that in a few short minutes, she'd be leaving this place behind, perhaps forever.

She rushed through the house, gathering her clothes and

shoes, folding everything into the only suitcase she possessed. Then she scoured the rooms for the things that meant the most to Werner and herself. The framed wedding picture. Check. The photo album from her childhood years. Love letters Werner had written to her. The silver necklace he'd given her for her birthday. The pipe she'd given him and that he enjoyed smoking so much. Check, check, check. Everything else would have to stay.

The chest of drawers they'd bought with his first paycheck after their marriage. Her grandmother's antique long-case clock. The crockery that was a wedding gift from Werner's parents. The monogrammed silverware.

She snuck two single spoons into the suitcase and closed it with tears in her eyes. The one-hour window drew to a close, and she found herself sitting atop the crammed suitcase and dreading Becker's return.

# CHAPTER 11

Sabine jumped at the awaited, and yet utterly unexpected, knock on the door. She glanced at her wristwatch, cursing the early arrival of her tormentor. Not more than fifty minutes had passed since Kriminalkommissar Becker had left the house. Her legs trembling, she made her way to the door somehow, without toppling over.

She smoothed her sweaty palms down her skirt and steeled herself for what would happen next as she opened the door.

Her jaw dropped to the floor at the sight of her neighbor.

Lily loped into the sitting room, swirling around to take everything in, before she came to a stand and scrunched up her nose. "I'm so sorry for all of this."

"You? You are sorry? It was your idea in the first place to recruit me to work for them!" Sabine managed to keep her voice sufficiently low so the other neighbors wouldn't hear her through the thin walls.

"Me? No." Lily gave a sharp laugh, shaking her head. "It was Becker's idea. But you should really have accepted my offer when I first told you about it. Nothing would have happened to Werner."

"What do you know about Werner?" Sabine struggled to remain calm.

"No more than you do. Anyway, I came over to say I'm sorry for how things developed for you, and…" Lily seemed to be searching for words. "…and to give you a word of advice. Do whatever Becker asks, give him the information he wants, and your life will be so much better than before."

A dark suspicion sprouted in Sabine's heart. Had Lily been the one to suggest Werner be arrested to assure Sabine's collaboration? "Go. Leave my house!" Sabine snapped, seething inside with a strong urge to wrap her hands around the woman's skinny neck and squeeze until she stopped breathing. For good.

Smirking, Lily turned on her heel and flounced out of the house.

Hatred, grief and desperation burned in Sabine's chest as she sank once again to the floor, looking at the lone suitcase standing in the entrance hall. Her life reduced to fifty by twenty inches. Never once had she believed this kind of thing could happen to her. Hadn't she slept well in the treacherous security of not getting involved with politics and keeping her mouth shut?

Minutes later she heard a pounding on the front door again. Her wristwatch attested that the given hour was over, and she almost admired the Kriminalkommissar for his punctuality. The desolation of her impasse weighing heavily on her shoulders, she opened the front door for the third time on this cold but sunny March morning.

Becker greeted her with the bright smile of a smitten lad and she half expected him to produce a bouquet of flowers from behind his back. Obviously this was wishful thinking, because the only things behind his back were five fierce-looking fellows in SS uniforms.

"Ah, you're ready to leave," Becker said with an exaggerated polite bow even as he motioned for the SS men to come inside. They carried strange-looking canisters and disappeared upstairs.

Sabine remained frozen in place, unable to make her legs move, when she heard heavy steps and slurping sounds above her head. She pressed a hand to her chest, feeling more than a bit embarrassed at the thought of five strange men rummaging through her private drawers.

Embarrassment turned into terror when the men trampled down the stairs, pouring an acid-smelling liquid on her freshly cleaned stairs. Sabine gagged, and then gagged some more when her brain recognized the smell.

"Wh...what are they doing?" she asked Becker, who patiently stood by her side, giving a contented smile at the spectacle unfolding in front of him.

"Making things look real."

*Real for what?* His plan to pretend her house had been bombed came crashing back and she shook her head in mute denial.

Becker ignored her and watched his men complete their work, before he took a matchbox from his pocket and offered it to her, "Would you like to do the honors?"

Sabine shook her head in bewilderment. She would not light up her own house. Becker, seeming not to care either way, lit the match and tossed it into the puddle of petrol. "It's an irony of fate, isn't it?"

"What is?" Sabine's brain felt like mash.

"That the home of a fireman would fall prey to fire," Becker chuckled and grabbed her elbow. "It's time to leave, Frau Mahler."

A strange gratitude crept through her for his unforgiving grip on her arm. Otherwise, she would have turned to rush inside and…and what?

Sabine's insides went numb. She lost all notion of time or place, but soon found herself sitting in the passenger seat of the black Gestapo vehicle, her suitcase neatly stowed in the trunk.

The vehicle lurched into motion and she couldn't resist looking back at the place she and Werner had once called home as black smoke began to rise skyward. A sob for the things she'd been forced to leave behind threatened to burst from her throat, and she swallowed it down, holding her chin high as her fingernails dug deep into the flesh of her palms.

How much more would she be required to give up before they returned Werner to her?

Unfazed by her distress, Becker said in his usual cold voice, "Don't worry about the housing assignment. I'll take care of everything. Unfortunately, I won't be able to drive you all the way to Frau Klausen's place since she might become suspicious. Here's the address." He handed her a sheet of paper with the insignia of the official housing agency. Two blocks from the address, he stopped to let her out of the vehicle and said, "Good luck. And don't forget to report to Fräulein Kerber twice a week."

Then he left her standing at the corner and his automobile sped away.

# CHAPTER 12

S abine walked the two blocks with her heavy suitcase in hand. Should she consider herself lucky that Becker had given her the opportunity to rescue her dearest things before torching her house?

The cold gusts of early March crept beneath her great-coat, making her yearn for the warm knitted blanket handed down from her grandmother. Gone up in flames.

Sabine shrugged. It didn't help to wallow in self-pity, because she needed to stay strong for Werner. She stopped in front of a huge apartment building, so different from the street of little row houses where she lived – *used to live*, she corrected herself.

Most of the buildings in the area still stood upright, although even the best-looking ones showed obvious signs of bombing damage. It was such a shame. And why did those damned Allies have to bomb Berlin to rubble? Couldn't they fight this war the old-fashioned way, soldier against soldier? Leaving the civilian population out of it?

Sabine pressed the bell and the electric buzzer sounded. She wondered that the door opener still worked with all the blackouts and shaky electricity in the city. The Klausen apartment was on the third floor, and Sabine dragged the heavy suitcase upstairs, heaving like a locomotive by the time she finally reached the landing.

As if by magic, a door opened and an elderly lady stepped out asking, "And you are?"

"Sabine Mahler, the new lodger," she said and extended her hand.

The woman eyed her suspiciously, blatantly ignoring Sabine's extended hand. "Who sent you?"

"The housing office assigned me to live here," Sabine said, fumbling the official sheet of paper from her purse.

"Not with me." The unfriendly woman stepped back and slammed the door in Sabine's face. Only then did Sabine notice the door sign that said *Weber*. She turned to look at the two other doors on the landing and finally knocked on the one that said *Klausen*.

It took a while, before she heard footsteps and the clicking sound of the metal plate behind the peephole. Several seconds passed and Sabine feared the door would never open, but it finally did.

"You?" Frau Klausen asked, an expression of utter disbelief on her face.

"I'm sorry, Frau Klausen. I was bombed out and the housing office assigned me to live with you," Sabine recited her rehearsed charade.

"Well, if that *isn't* a coincidence. Come in." Frau Klausen stepped out of the way and pointed at the small couch, worn to threads by many years of heavy use.

*Great! She doesn't buy my cover story.* Despite groaning inwardly, she plastered a smile on her face. "I'm so sorry for the inconvenience... Believe me, I didn't ask for this. I'd rather have stayed in my own place."

"When did you say your house was destroyed?" Frau Klausen asked, as she closed and locked the door.

*When? Truth be damned.* She hadn't thought about that part of the story and searched her brain for the latest news about air raids in Berlin and hoped to get the location right. "Four nights ago, in Steglitz."

"You told everyone your husband was in an accident. But in fact, your house was bombed? Where is he now?"

*God, why does this woman have to be so perceptive? And suspicious?* Sabine's palms dampened as she realized that from now on she had to guard every single word she spoke and keep track of each and every lie. "He...he got injured during the raid and..." Sabine squeezed a tear out of her eye. "He...died..."

"When did this happen?" the older woman asked, her eyes narrowing. Thankfully, the appearance of a young blonde woman, who was the spitting image of Frau Klausen – and sporting a pregnancy bump – rescued Sabine from answering. A wave of hurt and jealousy engulfed Sabine and for a moment she pondered turning on her heel and running away.

She couldn't possibly live in the same place with a happily expecting woman. Not when her own...she shook off the sad thoughts and forced a smile on her face when the other woman said, "Hello, I'm Ursula Herrmann. Frau Klausen is my mother."

"Sabine Mahler."

"I'm sorry for your loss," Ursula said, giving her mother a stern look. "Please make yourself at home and don't hesitate to ask should you need anything." After the animosity shown by the usually kind Frau Klausen, it was refreshing to see a genuine smile on Ursula's face.

"Thank you for making room in your apartment for me. I really appreciate this," Sabine said.

"We are always eager to comply with the requests the Reich imposes on us to best serve the war effort," Frau Klausen said in a stilted manner, and Sabine got the impression the older woman would just as soon strangle whoever had assigned a stranger into her home.

"Follow me," Frau Klausen said, leading the way through the sitting room and opening a door on the far side. "This is where you will be staying. I'm going to say this once and I hope I don't have to say it again. It would be better for people to believe we have never met prior to today."

*Never met?* Sabine thought that a strange request, but she didn't ask for an explanation and agreed, "Your house. Your rules."

A small smile appeared on Frau Klausen's lips and she said, "I see we understand each other. And since we're talking about rules. I expect you to keep your room tidy and share in the cleaning of the common areas."

Sabine nodded.

"And…" Frau Klausen gave a side glance at her daughter in the sitting room, before she continued, "This is a decent household and there will be no male visitors in my house. Is that clear?"

"Very clear," Sabine said, wondering why the older woman was concerned about male visitors with a woman who supposedly had been widowed the day before. And did that rule apply to Ursula's husband as well? She bit her tongue to keep from asking questions, since Frau Klausen's thinned lips indicated this was a non-discussable topic.

Not that she intended to receive any other man than Werner – and for the official record he was dead. Were dead men allowed to visit? She suppressed the small smile that wanted to spread, and called herself to order. His situation was too dire to joke about.

Frau Klausen left her to her own devices a few moments later and Sabine retired to her new bedroom, lying down on the bed fighting the cold hand of desolation forcing its grip on her.

# CHAPTER 13

T he next day at work Sabine returned from her lunch break to see Frau Klausen's station empty. Since Kriminalkommissar Becker's brilliant plan to have her move in with the suspect, the older woman had closed up and stopped talking to Sabine altogether. After getting up this morning it had been like walking on eggshells, the fragile tension inside the apartment about to explode at any moment.

Why, she had no idea. Maybe Frau Klausen really was a devious traitor and had somehow gotten a whiff of Sabine's new job as a Gestapo informer.

Caught between a potentially dangerous organization of subversives and the Gestapo holding her husband hostage, Sabine wanted to scream. Obviously she couldn't do so at work, even when the notion of having a nervous break-down followed by amnesia definitely held some merit.

She'd never wanted to get involved, let alone be drawn into the middle of a muddled conspiracy. Deep in thought, she finished assembling another batch of standard-issue Karabiner rifles and jumped at the voice of her superior.

"Frau Mahler, this is your new coworker, Fräulein Schenk."

She glanced up with confusion, noticing a rather young girl, barely of age, standing beside Herr Meier. A sliver of hope appeared on the horizon. If Frau Klausen had been arrested or was dead... With bated breath Sabine asked, "What happened to Frau Klausen?"

"She asked to be transferred to another department, where she didn't have to stand all day. Given her age, I granted her request."

Anger and relief fought for dominance. Somehow she needed to squeeze compromising information out of that lady, preferably in an inconspicuous manner. Maybe not having to work together would actually help?

While teaching yet another new employee the way of things, Sabine spent most of the day coming up with ways to gain Frau Klausen's confidence, but by the time she clocked out and headed to her new home, she still had no idea what to do.

She hated herself for ceding Becker so much control over her, but then, she couldn't simply walk away and let her husband rot in hell. And the Gestapo thug used such intimate knowledge to his advantage. Sabine had officially become a spy, just like Lily.

The urge to spit on the street nearly got the better of her, but she remained in control, plastering a ladylike smile on her face and feeling for her immaculate hairdo. No, appearances had to be kept up by any means. She wouldn't give anyone the satisfaction of seeing her break down.

Still, the lying, cheating and deceiving weighed heavily on her chest, even as she comforted herself with the knowledge that she didn't share her body with random men the way Lily did. A chill shook her shoulders. What would she do if Becker demanded that she be unfaithful to her husband? Would she acquiesce in order to save Werner? Could she?

The tremble ran all across her body and she wrapped the woolen scarf tighter around her shoulders, although she knew the chill wasn't caused by the icy wind. She shoved the distressing thoughts aside and started counting. Counting always helped her to calm down.

When she arrived in front of the building, the nosy neighbor, Frau Weber, appeared out of nowhere. "Good evening. Frau Mahler it is, right?"

"Yes, and you must be Frau Weber."

The older woman nodded. "So, you've moved in with the Klausens. Last year, there were strange things going on in their apartment. I could have sworn I heard a male voice. Frau Klausen was with her sister for a while, and the two girls Ursula and Anna shamelessly exploited her absence."

They reached the third floor and Sabine feebly protested, "Frau Weber...I..."

But Frau Weber wouldn't be stopped in her torrent of gossip. "Can you imagine that I had to call on the police? I was so worried about the safety of the people living here." Frau Weber pressed a hand to her bosom. "...And now Ursula is pregnant. Don't you think it strange that she became pregnant right after those mysterious things happened? And she won't tell..."

Sabine had heard enough. The reason why Frau Klausen

71

had insisted they both pretend they'd never seen each other before was becoming clear as crystal. "Frau Weber, with all due respect, but I'm not interested in your gossip about the people friendly enough to lodge me after my own house was bombed. I like to tend to my own business. Good evening." She opened the apartment door with her key and left the stupefied woman standing on the landing. Once inside, she almost bumped into Ursula, walking out of the kitchen.

"Don't get all fussed up over her," Ursula said and after a glance on Sabine's clueless face added, "Sorry, I couldn't help but overhear the fit you threw with our neighbor, Frau Weber. She's one of the worst gossip-blabbers I've ever had the misfortune to meet."

"Aww...thanks." Sabine wondered how much of the gossip was true. Not that she meant to stick her nose into others' affairs, but now the missing husband and the side blow about the decent household made sense.

"Would you like a cup of tea?" Ursula asked her.

"Yes, please." Sabine removed her coat, hanging it on the coat tree before joining Ursula in the kitchen.

"It's funny, isn't it, that you and my mother work in the same factory but have never met each other before?" Ursula asked as she handed Sabine a full cup of tea.

Sabine gasped and almost spilled the hot liquid across her hand. "It is, isn't it? Your mother works in a different department, though."

Ursula didn't reply, but flopped with a heavy sigh onto the chair opposite Sabine's. At least her bulging stomach was now out of sight and Sabine didn't have to swallow down the painful memories that assailed her every time she saw a pregnant woman.

"I'll be glad when I can finally quit my job. The work at the prison is so tiresome," Ursula said, leaning back to massage her stomach.

Sabine knew she should stop watching, but she couldn't tear her eyes away from the happy woman across from her, smiling as she laid a hand on her bump. It hurt so much. Just being in Ursula's presence ripped the fragile scars on her soul apart, opening up the old wound. After her second miscarriage two years ago, she hadn't been able to conceive another baby.

"I should lie down; I'm feeling unwell," Sabine lied and fled into the safety of her room, whishing Werner were there to soothe her and hold her close.

She missed him terribly, and if today were any indication of the success of her spying activities, then she'd never see him again. The unfairness of life tugged at every cell until the tears escaped and she sobbed herself to sleep.

# CHAPTER 14

S abine had barely closed her eyes when the shrill screech of the air raid sirens tore her awake. She sat up straight on the bed, her eyes blind in the complete darkness of the room with the blackout curtains drawn.

She fumbled for the switch of the nightlight, still not completely familiar in the strange room. When she finally found the switch and bathed the room in dim light, the sirens stopped wailing, and she scrambled from the bed, slipping into a woolen jacket that hung ready across the back of a chair.

In the sitting room she ran into Ursula, coming sleepily from her room, dressed in a long nightgown and a woolen jacket, just like Sabine. There was no time to get properly dressed, because the gruesome shrilling of the sirens started up again, indicating *akute Luftgefahr*, immediate danger.

Ursula and Sabine slipped into their shoes and grabbed the suitcase beside the door, stocked with extra clothes, food, and water. A night in the shelter could get rather long.

One should think that after so many years of being bombed almost on a nightly basis, people would get used to it.

Wrong.

Chills of terror still ran down Sabine's limbs every time the sirens sounded, and the queasy feeling in her stomach wouldn't let up until she heard the all-clear signal.

"We need to get to the basement," Sabine hissed in a shaky voice.

"No. Shelter. Follow me." Ursula hurried downstairs, Sabine on her heels. On every landing, more people poured out of their apartments, scurrying like frightened mice to the safety of the shelter.

Sabine dragged the small suitcase behind and suddenly remembered Frau Klausen. "Where's your mother?" she yelled at Ursula, who didn't falter in her steps.

She shouted back, "Over at my sister's, I suppose."

In any case, there was no time to stop and worry. Sabine shrugged, thinking it ironic that the apartment building where she lodged now, because her own house had been destroyed by the SS, might succumb to real enemy bombs.

In her district people usually sought shelter in their basements, but here crowds of people fled to the next public shelter, a *Hochbunker*. The bunker was a huge concrete building, sufficient to host five hundred people. Even the sight of that many people that would share the space with her for the next hours frightened Sabine.

Ursula led the way to a corner, fitted with three mattresses and blankets, and pointed at one of them, "Take this space. It was Anna's but since she moved away, it's yours now."

Sabine had never been in such a huge public shelter

before and she wished for the small confines of her own basement. People always argued the *Hochbunker* were safer than the cellars. The house above could burn to the ground and suck all the oxygen out of the basement, effectively suffocating those seeking shelter in there.

But seeing the multitude of people squeezing inside, before the doors were firmly locked, made her queasy stomach revolt and she barely managed to keep the remains of her dinner down. The two women settled on the mattresses, both of them consumed by their own worries and fears, when Sabine noticed Ursula's painful moans.

"Are you alright?"

"Yes...ouch...I...guess..."

Sabine peered in the semi-darkness at Ursula's damp face and then her eyes lowered to the other woman's bump, where visible contractions pulled at her belly. *Oh, God. No. She's...how far along?*

"You need to relax and breathe," Sabine said, helping Ursula to sit on the mattress and lean against the wall.

"Relax?" Ursula murmured, the effort of trying to do just that showing on her creased forehead. "You'd think I'd be used to the air raids by now, since they happen so often."

Sabine gave a short laugh. "I don't think anyone ever gets used to being awakened by the earth exploding around them."

A small smile appeared on Ursula's face, until the next contraction wiped it away. "I'm frightened," she whispered. "I'm only in my seventh month."

"Nothing will happen," Sabine said, hoping she spoke the truth. Premature babies happened all the time, but everyone knew that those babies in fact weren't always delivered early. Probably the best thing to do was to distract Ursula from her fears, by talking to her.

"I'm grateful that you've received me so kindly in your home. It must be difficult to share it with a stranger." Sabine retrieved a bottle of water from the suitcase, poured some into the lid that could be used as cup and handed it to Ursula.

"Thank you." Ursula closed her eyes, drinking the water, her face showing a pensive expression. "Our apartment used to be full with my parents and the four of us, and I longed for the day when I could move out. But now that it's only Mutter and myself, it feels lonely."

"Tell me about your siblings," Sabine encouraged her.

"Well, my sister Anna used to live there until several weeks ago, when she was offered employee housing at the *Charité* clinic. She works there as a nurse. My mother didn't like the idea, but Anna convinced her that it was safer…with the blackouts and the air raids…" Ursula smiled, and the contractions seemed to ease up. "Then there's my brother Richard. He's eighteen and we haven't seen him in almost two years, since the day he was drafted. Currently he's fighting somewhere in Poland. And Lotte, the youngest. She's…dead. Contracted typhus." Ursula scrunched up her nose but didn't look very sad at the loss of her sister. "What about you?"

Sabine stowed the water bottle between the two mattresses. So far, Ursula's family was completely unremarkable. Nothing remotely noteworthy. "Me? I'm an only child. My parents moved to Freiburg a couple of years ago, because of my father's job. So I don't get to see them very often."

77

"Oh, I couldn't imagine not seeing my family at least once a week. As much as I loathe them sometimes, I also need to have them around. Especially, Anna. She's my confidante, my best friend, and my moral compass to keep me straight."

"That's what my husband is…was," Sabine said, unable to hold back the feeling of nostalgia that swept across her at the thought of Werner. She literally ached from missing him. His warmth. His laugh. His touch.

"I'm sorry," Ursula said, grabbing her hand. "It must be so hard for you. What was he like?"

"Werner?" Sabine mentioned his name and felt the wound in her soul open a bit more. *What am I supposed to say?*

She took her time answering and then softly revealed as much of the truth as she could. "Werner was a wonderful man and my best friend. I still can't believe he's gone, and there's a little part of me that still hopes he will survive all of this."

"I thought he died in the bombing?" Ursula asked, shocking Sabine to the core.

"He did. It's just, his body still hasn't been found. One moment he was alive and the next…" Sabine sobbed, not sure what flustered her more, the fact that he'd been kidnapped by the Gestapo or that every word she spoke to Ursula was a lie. To redeem her conscience with some bits of truth, she gave Ursula a weak smile. "I have many good memories with him, and I'm grateful for every single day I spent with him."

Sabine couldn't help but voice the question that had

been burning on her tongue for the past few days. "What about the father of your baby? Where is he?"

Ursula stiffened and pulled her hand away. "He died in action at the front."

Stunned at the cold and unemotional manner in which Ursula delivered this information, Sabine got the message loud and clear. She didn't welcome the topic of the baby's father.

Sabine closed her eyes and imagined Werner there with her, holding her in his arms and keeping her safe. All the while the tension around her mounted with the reverberating echo of the shells coming closer to their location.

# CHAPTER 15

Several minutes later, Ursula spoke again. "So many people disappear these days. Without a trace. I worry about them. Mother says it's the pregnancy making me overly emotional, but...I can't help but wonder what happens to those people who can't get to a shelter on nights like these."

Sabine gave Ursula a quizzical look and asked, "Do you know people who are stuck outside and can't get to a shelter?"

Ursula looked at her steadily for a moment and then nodded slowly. "Yes."

"Who are they? People who live in your apartment building?" A wave of horror washed over Sabine as she imagined an elderly lady unable to hurry down the stairs.

"Just people." Ursula said nothing for a long time, and then another impact came, and the two women huddled together as dirt trickled down. When the dust settled,

Ursula sighed and shook her head. "I hope everyone is alright."

"Who are you talking about? Is there anyone of your family out there?" Sabine was getting worried about Ursula's evasive statements.

Ursula lowered her voice to a whisper that was barely audible and confided in her, "Sometimes, I hide people."

"Hide?" Sabine gasped. So it was true – Frau Klausen and her daughter were devious traitors to the Reich.

Ursula glanced around, her eyes flickering with fear. "I shouldn't have told you since it's really nothing. Some people don't have a place to live."

Sabine wondered what kind of people didn't have a place to live and why they wouldn't simply go to the authorities and ask for a housing assignment. Except if…they weren't law-abiding citizens. Images of cold-blooded axe-swinging murderers swamped her mind, fueled by the knowledge that Ursula worked as a prison guard. Rapists, thieves, and blackmailers of the worst kind. Big, strong men who could break her neck with a single move of their hand. Goosebumps covered her skin and she willed the images away.

"A…aren't you afraid?" Sabine asked.

"Every single day," Ursula admitted, crouching back onto the mattress and taking another sip of water.

"But…why do you help these people if you're so afraid of them? Shouldn't they be arrested and go to prison instead?"

Ursula's eyes went wide and once again she glanced around, as if any moment someone could appear out of the shadows and swing his axe. There it was again, that horrific image. "I'm not afraid of *them*, but…" A shudder racked

Ursula's thin shoulders and she turned her head away, indicating the conversation was over.

Sabine nodded her understanding even though she didn't understand a thing. Why would someone like Ursula, a beautiful woman, pregnant with her first child, risk her life for...for...outlaws? Enemies of the Reich?

Maybe Kriminalkommissar Becker was right and the Klausens really were devious, deplorable people masquerading as rightful citizens. Who could they be hiding from the authorities? Escaped prisoners? People evading justice? Criminals?

Her stomach grew queasy until hot and cold flashes rushed down her skin as she was reminded of one of Werner's anecdotes. Women and children herded outside by SS troopers. Shot. Without trial or defense.

Guilt swamped Sabine. Maybe Ursula was hiding innocent people? People that would otherwise be shot on the spot just for the simple crime of their existence? Now she wished Ursula hadn't confided in her.

Sabine sighed. She hadn't adopted the policy not to get involved because she was unscrupulous; on the contrary. *What I don't know won't hurt me – or anyone else.* Apparently, this motto held true no longer, not since the Gestapo had burst into her and Werner's lives.

The lines of right and wrong had blurred and while the bombs still dropped on Berlin, she wrestled with her next steps. Could she really take it onto her conscience to feed a pregnant woman to the pack of wolves?

# CHAPTER 16

Sabine entered the exclusive bakery and glanced around, finding Lily sitting at a small table near one of the windows. Or more to the point, what was left of the windows. As in most buildings, the glass had been shattered and replaced with fabric, cardboard or wood.

She made her way through the other patrons and took a seat, trying to find a smile for the woman who had turned her world upside down.

"There you are," Lily said with a definite attitude. "I was afraid you'd stand me up."

"Sorry I'm late. I didn't realize how long it would take me to get here from across town." Sabine eyed the *Franzbrötchen*, a sweet bun, on Lily's plate, next to a cup of brown liquid. *Ersatzkaffee* was a detestable liquid and Sabine had long given up coffee in favor of herbal tea. But the scent that now wafted toward her nostrils was...unmistakably... real delicious coffee. Her mouth watered and she involuntarily inhaled deeply.

Lily saw the wistful expression on Sabine's face and snapped her fingers. Moments later the waitress appeared beside her table. "What can I bring you?"

"Another coffee, with sugar, please."

*Sugar?* Even bakeries were constantly short of sugar and had resorted to adapting their recipes to include less of the prized white substance. Usually to the detriment of flavor.

Sabine settled onto the chair across from Lily, her hand shooting up to control her hairdo. If nothing else remained stable in her world, she could at least hold on to looking the part.

"Do you have information for me?" Lily asked, taking a sip from her coffee.

"I'm afraid not much…Frau Klausen is very tight-lipped," Sabine said, omitting the confession Ursula had made in the bunker.

Lily shook her head, putting a cigarette into the long holder. "You still don't get it, do you?"

"Get what?"

"This…what we're doing…it is a big deal."

"A big deal?" Sabine asked confused.

"Yes, we're helping the Führer to rid the Reich of our enemies. Subversives, traitors, undesirables. We're of invaluable service to our country. You should be proud they've chosen you for this work."

Sabine didn't feel proud at all. Aghast would be a better word to describe her emotions. Ever since the day she'd agreed to Kriminalkommissar Becker's requests, she'd been loathing herself. Herself, her task, and her willingness to doom other people to save her husband's skin.

Raised as a Roman Catholic, Christian notions of

altruism had quickly fled her life when the war – and with it, the struggle for survival – had started. Killing others and believing in Jesus didn't go hand in hand – at least in Sabine's world.

But looking the other way was one thing, betraying people to the Gestapo entirely different. A wave of nausea hit her and she asked, "Don't you ever feel bad for the people you turn in?"

Lily rolled her eyes. "Of course not. They're traitors."

"Not all of them. What about the innocents who get caught up in your little game? Like my husband? He didn't do anything wrong and was still arrested."

"Werner is an unfortunate accidental victim," Lily leaned forward and whispered, "I'm sorry about him, because he's a nice man. But – it's all *your* fault. Nothing would have happened to him if you had been cooperative."

Sabine quickly took a sip from her coffee to keep herself from saying something stupid. A burning sensation struck her tongue and she winced. She set down the cup in as lady-like a fashion as she could and bestowed a smile on Lily – the very woman she'd started to hate with every fiber of her soul. Shudders rolled down her back as she remembered what had happened the last time she'd given Lily a piece of her mind. Although – what else could the Gestapo take from her? Since they'd already taken her husband and her home, there wasn't much left.

*They can take your life.*

Lily was even more shallow and self-centered than she looked with her immaculate make-up, the flower in her hair and the elegant cigarette holder between her manicured fingers. The only goal Sabine had in mind at this point was ending this meeting as soon as possible, while doing everything to keep her husband alive.

Sabine swallowed her disgust and said, "Frau Klausen is as tight-lipped as ever, but I'm starting to build a relationship with her daughter Ursula. A few nights ago in the bunker, she was so upset that she confided in me that she sometimes hides people."

"Well, that is a start!" Lily clapped her hands, only to bestow charming smiles upon two officers sitting at a table nearby. She lowered her voice and continued, "It's nothing we don't already know, but it shows you're gaining her trust. Which is good, very good. Work harder to secure Ursula's trust. Get her to include you in her resistance activities. Get her to introduce you to others."

Sabine's stomach churned at the thought of deceiving the kind woman in such a way. "I don't know if that's the best approach…"

Lily gave her a hard look. "It's the only approach that will yield the required information. For God's sake forget your uncalled-for scruples and do as I say. Never forget, your husband is languishing somewhere while you debate the morality of turning traitors in for their rightful punishment."

Sabine stared at Lily as the truth of the evil woman's words struck her like jagged stones. She had to stick by her choice. It was either her conscience or Werner's life. Sometimes sacrifices must be made, and her conscience was one of them.

# CHAPTER 17

A few weeks later, Sabine was sitting in the kitchen preparing tea, when the bell rang.

"I'll open it," Frau Klausen said and disappeared.

Sabine didn't give it much thought since she never received visitors anyway. Several minutes later, Frau Klausen returned with a beautiful blonde woman and a dark-blond bearded man in tow.

"This is Sabine," Frau Klausen said, introducing them, "our bombed-out refugee. And this is my second daughter, Anna, and her boyfriend, Peter Wolf."

"Nice to meet you," Anna said, giving Sabine a friendly smile.

"The same to you," Sabine answered and extended her hand. The moment she shook Anna's hand, she knew the smile had been fake. Anna's palpable dislike for her crackled in the air.

The man called Peter Wolf was huge, with the build of a wrestler and he had the most amazing glacial blue eyes. But despite his pleasant exterior she felt the same carefully hidden vigilance in his demeanor. Both of them were more than the eye could see.

Under his piercing gaze, Sabine felt like an insect under a microscope. No, he was definitely hiding something. It wasn't anything he said or did, but rather, just a feeling she got.

Maybe he was also part of the underground network? Could he be the person in charge and she'd been spying on the wrong sister? Sabine tabled that thought for later and tried to become invisible to the others, hoping to gather some valuable information.

"Where's Ursula?" Anna asked her mother.

"Queuing for rations," Frau Klausen said, shrugging. "Poor girl. So far along, and now the entire household rests on her shoulders. I would rather see her safe in the country with Lydia, but she insists that she's needed here."

Sabine pricked up her ears, hoping Frau Klausen would spill a few facts about why exactly Ursula was needed here. Anna and her boyfriend were surely in the know. But Peter Wolf slashed Sabine's hopes when he asked Frau Klausen for the hand of her daughter in marriage.

*So romantic!* For a moment, Sabine forgot that she was here to spy on them.

Frau Klausen, though, didn't seem to be pleased at all because she plopped down on the kitchen chair and stared at her daughter and future son-in-law, laughing uncontrollably.

A prickle of fear settled in Sabine's chest, as she'd never seen Frau Klausen showing her emotions in such an exuberant way.

"We'll take my mother to her room," Anna said with a hard glance at Sabine, and Sabine dutifully stepped out of the way.

*Damn it! Just when she might be letting down her guard.* Sabine wouldn't give up so easily, and tiptoed to Frau Klausen's bedroom, sharpening her ears. The hysterical giggling stopped, but just when Sabine inched closer, the radio in the bedroom blared a program with folk songs. *Double damn it!*

The Klausens were incredibly careful. The entire apartment and the phone line were bugged, and yet the Gestapo had never picked up anything remotely helpful in their quest to capture the head of the underground organization.

In fact, the only time Ursula or her mother had ever given Sabine any indication that things were not as they seemed was during that first night in the shelter. Since that time, no mention of hiding people or helping individuals avoid detection and capture by the authorities had escaped Ursula's lips.

Sabine leaned up against the door, straining to hear what was going on behind the wood partition, when suddenly, the door swung open and she stumbled. Righting herself, she turned and looked up into the blazing eyes of Peter Wolf.

*Wolf, what a fitting name.* She instinctively took a step back, afraid he'd pounce at her and bite down on her throat. Her heart hammering frantically against her ribs, she struggled to come up with a believable excuse. Something. Anything.

"What the hell!" He pulled the door shut and took a

threatening step toward her. "What are you doing? Eaves-dropping?"

Sabine feebly shook her head. "No, I just...I've never seen Frau Klausen so upset and I thought...well, I only want to help."

As excuses went, it was weak, and she could tell by the look on Peter's face that he didn't believe a single word she'd just said. He advanced on her, forcing her backwards until her back hit the wall. His irate stare bore through her with intense heat. She seemed to shrivel into a dwarf and held her breath, waiting for him to kill her right there and then. Everything about him screamed danger.

"Tell me why you were listening at the door," he demanded, his breath moving over her face.

Sabine swallowed and struggled to inhale. "I only wanted to help...Frau Klausen and Ursula have been so kind...having me in their home..."

"I don't believe you." He searched her eyes and said with a calm, yet ominous voice, "If you hurt my family, I will kill you. That is a promise."

Sabine didn't have a chance to reply because a knock came on the apartment door. For a moment she thought Peter Wolf would ignore it and continue to threaten her, but he cursed beneath his breath and removed his hands from beside her shoulders.

"Remember what I said," he cautioned her as he headed for the front door.

Sabine stood there crestfallen, while Peter opened the door and greeted a young girl around the age of twelve who had a small cloth-wrapped loaf of bread in her hands.

"Could you see that Frau Klausen gets this? It's from my mother."

"Thank you. I'll make sure she gets it. Take care going home," Peter said in such a friendly voice, as if he hadn't just threatened to kill someone.

"I will."

To avoid another confrontation with this disquieting man, Sabine darted into her room, shutting and locking the door. It seemed she'd now placed herself between the Gestapo and whoever this Peter was working for.

For a fleeting moment she considered disappearing. Pack her meager belongings and leave the country. But, as soon as the thought arose, she tamped it down. She couldn't leave. Not without Werner.

She could never live with the guilt of having abandoned the one person who loved her unconditionally.

No. Regardless of how difficult it was, she had to stay the course.

# CHAPTER 18

May arrived with sunshine and blossoming trees. Even in a devastated Berlin, people gathered hope again. Nothing looked as bleak as it had during the cold and dark winter.

Sabine dreaded her next meeting with Lily, since she had nothing to tell her. She battled with herself whether it would be good or bad to tell Lily about Peter Wolf and his threats. It might appease the Gestapo when she gave them something, or it might infuriate them because they thought she'd been found out and wouldn't be useful to them anymore.

But she needed to give them something, since they wouldn't wait patiently for much longer. During the last two meetings, Lily had dropped remarks about Sabine's sub-par performance and that she needed to come up with something substantial soon. Real soon.

But how?

The tension inside the Klausen household had never

lessened since that fateful night when Peter and Anna had visited. Frau Klausen refused to even meet Sabine's eyes, and not even Ursula spoke to her anymore. No doubt, Peter had told them about their little encounter.

Sabine had been hoping to find a chance to speak with Ursula alone, to try to explain herself, but Ursula was never alone. It appeared as if the others were afraid of leaving her alone with Sabine.

Life in the apartment had become very depressing and uncomfortable. Sabine did her best to cope. She went to work, came home, went to bed, and then got up the next day and did it all over again.

In the darkness of the night, she cried herself to sleep, longing for her husband and silently cursing Lily for ever talking to her – cursing Kriminalkommissar Becker for his outrageous blackmail. Soon, she found herself looking constantly over her shoulder, sure some Gestapo lowlife would show up and abduct her as well.

Defying Lily's pressure to mingle with the Klausens, she usually kept to herself, leaving her bedroom door slightly ajar, so she could hear most of what they said. Not that they ever incriminated themselves.

In fact, their conversations had been so mundane, Sabine started to wonder whether the Gestapo was barking up the wrong tree and the Klausens were actually innocent. Still, she listened in on them every chance she got. However lately all the conversations revolved around Anna's and Peter's impending wedding, making Sabine even more depressed about her missing husband.

She wondered how fast they'd arranged for the necessary papers, remembering the huge amount of red tape she and Werner had had to work through to receive a marriage license. But that was none of her business. Nothing in this household was, and she cursed once again the fate that had catapulted her into the middle of this intrigue.

"So, will Lotte be able to make it?" Ursula asked her mother.

*Lotte? Isn't that the youngest sister, the dead one?* Sabine held her breath, hoping nobody would notice that she stood in the hallway readying herself to go outside and run some errands.

"Your sister is *dead*," Frau Klausen said, and then lowered her voice so Sabine couldn't understand her next words.

Probably an overload of emotion in a heavily pregnant woman. Since there was no answer, Sabine put on her hat, carefully draping it on her hair, and glanced at the image in the mirror. She took solace in the immaculate elegance of her appearance, even though she knew it was a silly thing to do. But what else did she have left as a remainder of normalcy and better times?

Shortly after Peter and Anna's wedding, Frau Klausen called Sabine into the kitchen. "Frau Mahler, I know we haven't been on the best terms lately, and I'm sorry for that." By the way the older woman pursed her lips, Sabine clearly noticed that she still mistrusted her. "My daughter and I are going to travel to Upper Bavaria for a few days and I want to entrust you with our apartment."

Relief rushed through Sabine. With the family gone, she wouldn't have to spy on them anymore. But the next moment, cold waves of shock hit her. With the family gone, the Gestapo might not need her services anymore, either.

"Upper Bavaria?" Sabine said, looking at Ursula and her belly in advanced pregnancy. "Such a long trip?"

"My sister is going to receive the Mother's Cross in Silver, and what better occasion to visit her than to celebrate this momentous occasion?" Frau Klausen said.

"That's indeed a prestigious award. Congratulations to your sister," Sabine said with a smile she hoped might be returned. It wasn't, but at least Frau Klausen was speaking to her again.

"Thank you. It has been quite some time since any of us have vacationed together in the country. I'm not looking forward to the train ride, but it will be nice to see my sister once again," Frau Klausen answered.

"I hope you all have a lovely time. When exactly are you leaving?"

"In two days," Peter answered her question as he walked into the kitchen, the suspicion barely concealed in his glacial blue eyes as he stared at her.

The day before the scheduled travel day, Sabine returned home from the munitions factory and noticed the tension thick in the air. Judging by the agitated voices, Ursula and her mother were having a fit over something.

"I'm staying," Ursula said in the same moment Sabine walked into the kitchen. When the two women saw her, they stopped talking. Burning with curiosity to find out what they were fighting over, Sabine excused herself to the bedroom, leaving the door slightly ajar. By now she knew they wouldn't speak another word with Sabine in earshot.

She inched closer to the door, holding her breath as she

pressed her ear against the clearance between leaf and frame. The whispering between the two women became louder. Harsher. And after a few more heated exchanges, they'd dropped their caution altogether and Sabine could understand their words.

"You can't stay here. Not by yourself," Frau Klausen said.

"There is no one else to do it. I must stay."

"It's too risky. Why on earth can't you think of yourself and the baby first, just this once?" Frau Klausen's voice trembled with barely concealed sorrow.

"Because those people need me, Mutter." Ursula tried to calm her mother.

*Those people? The ones in hiding?* Sabine almost laughed out loud at the serendipity. Would the Klausens finally talk about the family secret?

"We need you, too…remember what happened to your sister Lotte." With those words Frau Klausen walked away and minutes later Sabine heard the front door snap close.

*What happened to Lotte? I thought she died of typhus?* The whole dead sister story stank. For days everyone had been talking about her as if she were still alive and now this warning? Sabine shrugged. She had more serious issues to worry about. Providing the Gestapo with the required information, for example.

Sabine squared her shoulders, a plan forming in her mind. She hated playing with the needs and worries of a pregnant woman, but Werner's life was at stake here. "God forgive me!" she whispered and stepped out of her room.

# CHAPTER 19

"Ursula, I don't mean to overstep here, but I overheard you talking about staying here rather than visiting your aunt, as planned," Sabine said, putting on a concerned smile.

"Mutter is just being stubborn." Ursula put out her lower lip, a gesture that made her look like a petulant child. Stubbornness seemed to run in the family.

"No, your mother is just worried about you," Sabine said, carefully forming the next sentence in her head. "You are so far along and so many things could go wrong at this stage."

Ursula's lower lip returned to its place and worry etched itself into her face. "You think so?"

Sabine nodded, hating herself for what she had to do next. Pushing through the pain and guilt she said, "Yes. I do. Usually I don't tell people, because the wounds are still fresh, but two years ago I lost two babies within a year's time." A sob bubbling up in her throat interrupted her, and she took a few moments to compose herself. Not daring to look at Ursula, she was thankful that the other woman didn't utter a word. "I...I was alone when it happened and I always ask myself if the babies could have been saved by a competent woman by my side." That last sentence was a lie.

"Oh my God! How awful! I'm so sorry for you," Ursula said, putting a hand on Sabine's arm. "I feel like a klutz now, parading my happy bump in front of you."

Tears sprung into Sabine's eyes, but strangely enough they seemed to stem more from Ursula's unexpected sympathy than from the grief Sabine had carried around with herself for so long. "I admit, it still hurts, but that is no reason to be jealous of you." *Of course it is!* "And I really think you should go with your mother; I couldn't stand it if..." Sabine dabbed at her eyes, before she continued. "Go visit your aunt and everything will be fine."

Ursula's face reflected a war with her emotions, each one fighting for dominance. Sabine waited patiently for a clue before she said, "If there is anything I can do to help or to ease your mind about why you feel you should stay here, I don't mind. I know my being here has been difficult for you and your mother and I'd like a chance to repay your kindness."

Ursula gave a short laugh. "Kindness? I think maybe that hasn't always been true." She thought for a moment and then shook her head a second time. "Thank you for the offer, but it's just too dangerous. I couldn't ask you to help."

"You are about to give birth within the month. If you can do whatever it is, then I can certainly do so as well. How dangerous could it be? Please, won't you let me help?" Sabine said, desperate to change Ursula's mind. This might be her one and only chance to get a foot into the under-ground organization – if it even existed.

Ursula looked at her for a long time before she slowly nodded. "I guess maybe you could help…"

"Anything. Just tell me what you need."

"It's nothing, really. But if you could get an urgent message to our priest in the morning…" Ursula said with a shy smile. Sabine wanted to slap her. All this mystery and evasiveness for a simple message to a priest? What kind of Charlie Chaplin slapstick was this?

"Well, that's not hard or dangerous. I'd be happy to deliver the message before work tomorrow morning," Sabine answered, doing her best to keep the disappointment out of her expression.

"Pfarrer Bernau lives in the small house adjacent to his church." Ursula took pen and paper and drew a map for Sabine with directions to the church and handed it to her, saying, "Are you sure you wouldn't mind doing this for me?"

"Not at all. I'll take it first thing in the morning and hand it over to Pfarrer Bernau. He should be there at that time, right?"

"Yes. He usually prepares mass in the mornings. I'll just write down the message and slide it under your bedroom door before I go to bed…"

"Fine with me."

Ursula gave Sabine the first real smile. "Thank you. I didn't want to stay here all on my own, even though I'm not sure travelling in my condition is the wisest course of action."

"Go and enjoy yourself. If nothing else, you'll be able to

get a good night's sleep down there that isn't disrupted by the nightly bombing raids."

Ursula chuckled, rubbing her stomach. "A night of undisturbed sleep sounds like paradise. Thank you again for your help."

"You're welcome. Now, if there's nothing else, I'm off to bed." Sabine returned to her room, barely able to contain her excitement over this turn of events. At least now she would have something substantial to tell Lily. Although a message to a priest wasn't the most compromising action in the world.

Soon enough sleep claimed her, and she barely cracked open half an eye when Frau Klausen and Ursula left before dawn. But then she remembered the message and jumped from her bed, scrambling to pick up the paper lying on the linoleum behind her bedroom door.

Excitement – and shame – burning up her face and ears, she glanced at the white envelope and turned it around. Nothing written anywhere. *Sealed!* Damn woman, wasn't sealing an envelope proof enough that its content was illicit?

Sabine needed to read the contents of the letter before she handed it over, or else she wouldn't have any information to give to Lily. But if the priest found out that she'd opened it, he wouldn't trust her. What could she do?

A new envelope came to her mind and she frantically searched the kitchen, the sitting room and even the second bedroom. Entering Frau Klausen's and Ursula's private space felt like a crime and she had the icky feeling of someone watching her. Carefully opening drawers and closets, she found – nothing. At long last her glance fell on the small bureau in the corner of the room.

*Locked!* Of course, they would lock up the bureau in their own home, as if someone would come and search for their secrets. Her neck hair stood on end and she giggled hysterically at her thoughts. Obviously, someone did search the Klausens' private room. Sabine sank onto the bed, covering her face with her hands as she realized what had become of her: a conniving treacherous snake.

With the envelope in hand, she gave up her search and walked into the kitchen to make tea before she had to leave for priest Bernau's church. Putting a kettle of water on the stove, she pondered her options. Should she telephone Kriminalkommissar Becker and ask him what to do? A wave of disgust rolled through her body and she decided that the less she saw of him, the better.

Or… might she just open the envelope and pretend the message had come without it? The priest might well believe it…or not. Sabine gave a heavy sigh. There was no solution to her problem.

The kettle whistled, and she glanced toward the stove, a broad smile spreading across her face. Apparently, there was a solution!

After pouring some of the boiling water into a cup for her morning tea, she poured the rest into a bowl and located a dishtowel. She held the envelope over the steaming bowl of water, trapping the steam with the towel, and waited for the glue holding the flap down to loosen.

Several minutes later, she turned the envelope over and rejoiced in her accomplishment when the last bit of glue was released from the paper. Her fingers trembling with nerves, she sat back and drank from her tea first. For the first time since Werner's disappearance, she saw a ray of hope.

Carefully, she removed the letter, making sure the envelope would look untampered with when she was done, smoothed out the message on the tabletop and began to read –

*Pfarrer Bernau,*

*Please forgive me but I cannot attend the choir practice at your church as I'll be travelling with my family. I apologize and look forward to attending next week.*

*Ursula Hermann*


"She must be joking!" Sabine yelled at the empty room, balling her hands into fists. Missing a choir practice? What exactly was so important or urgent about a stupid choir practice? Even if Ursula was the soloist, it didn't justify her allusions to people needing her.

Sabine searched the letter for hidden text, and she shook her head in despair when she didn't find any. The renewed hope sucked out of her, she placed the letter back into the envelope and carefully sealed the flap closed.

Minutes later she left the apartment to deliver the message. Maybe the priest could shed some light on this? Or maybe Ursula's overreaction was completely innocent and only due to her advanced stage of pregnancy?

Either way, she would have a word with Pfarrer Bernau.

# CHAPTER 20

S abine enjoyed the morning sunshine of May, her favorite month of the year. The chestnut trees lining the alley were in full blossom: flower umbels in white and soft pink adorned the trees, petals trickling to the ground with every breeze.

The chirping of blackbirds and other birds filled the air, almost like a choir filled the vast nave in a church. A few steps further on, she saw a squirrel scurrying up the trunk and then jumping precariously from branch to branch. Sabine smiled. Lots of life existed amidst the rubble, and neither the squirrel nor the birds seemed to have a single sorrow. One day all of this would end and life would return to normal. One day people could live again and not merely survive.

She arrived at the small and relatively new church: a plain white building, unlike the ostentatious Berlin Cathedral that was reminiscent of the glorious times in the fifteenth and sixteenth centuries.

Sabine crossed herself with holy water from the basin next to the door before stepping inside. Rays of sunshine shone through the plain, transparent altar windows – probably replacements for damaged stained glass – and danced across the light brown stone floor. In one of the dark wooden benches kneeled a few old women with gray hair, their head scarves tightly knotted beneath their chins.

But Pfarrer Bernau was nowhere to be seen. Remembering Ursula's instructions, Sabine left the church again and rounded the building to find the entrance to the small house next to it.

Her heart pounded more furiously the nearer she got to the door. She swallowed down her fear, shame and guilt before she knocked.

A gaunt man in his late forties, with warm brown eyes and dressed in a black suit, opened the door. "Good morning, how can I help you?"

"I'm looking for Pfarrer Bernau," she said, nervously running a hand across her hair.

"You found him." He gazed at her for several long moments and then said, "Please come inside."

His energy was of a man truly at peace with himself, and a sense of calmness overcame her. She had nothing to fear from him. "My name is Sabine Mahler, and Ursula Hermann has asked me to give you a message."

Worry etched itself into his brown eyes. "Does she feel unwell? Has something happened with the baby?"

"No, no. Ursula and her mother are travelling to visit Frau Klausen's sister for a few days. She was very upset and urged me to let you know." Sabine pulled the envelope from her pocket and handed it over to the priest.

Pfarrer Bernau nodded as he opened the envelope and read the letter inside. A frown appeared on his forehead and he seemed very concerned about the content of the message.

*A missed choir practice – really?* "Is something wrong, Pfarrer Bernau?" Sabine asked.

"No. It's just a minor inconvenience." The priest's expression didn't match his words, and Sabine decided to make a bold move.

"Ursula was so worried, she almost cancelled the entire trip to Upper Bavaria. I convinced her that was not for the best for her baby and agreed to fill in while she was away."

Pfarrer Bernau raised a brow, asking, "Fill in? Frau Hermann told you what she's been doing?"

Sabine nodded, stretching the truth as far as she could. "Yes, and I'm on your side. She told me about helping to hide people seeking refuge and a way out of Germany."

Pfarrer Bernau stared at her for several long moments and Sabine willed herself to appear confident and trustworthy. "Then Frau Hermann must really trust you. Confiding in the wrong persons can torpedo our entire network."

"I like to think we are friends," Sabine offered, tying to conceal the feeling of victory building up inside her.

"The timing of her departing Berlin is not ideal, since we had to postpone a few activities due to unforeseen circumstances," Pfarrer Bernau said, still scrutinizing Sabine.

"I understand and all I want to do is help." Sabine prayed she wouldn't blush at the blatant lie. Her heart squeezed tight. Deceiving a man of God – one more sin piled up on her existing mountain of transgressions.

"There is a young Jewish girl hiding in the Klausens'

allotment. Frau Hermann was supposed to bring her to the arranged meeting place and hand her over to someone else. Are you familiar with the allotment?"

"I am." Another lie. She knew about its existence and had seen the numbered key hanging on the keyboard in the apartment. "And I'm happy to perform Ursula's duties while she's gone. But I have never actually been at the allotments...Ursula deemed it too dangerous."

"That's probably right. You two showing up there together might have raised suspicions, but since the family is now on a trip, you can go there to tend the plants. Everyone in Berlin will understand the importance of taking care of the produce." A slight smile crossed Pfarrer Bernau's face.

"The perfect excuse – when shall I go there?" Sabine asked, taking an awful chance. In fact she had no idea where the allotment was.

"Not so fast, my daughter." Pfarrer Bernau looked at her carefully and asked, "Are you sure you wish to take this kind of risk? If you are discovered, you will be labeled a traitor, and we all know the Nazis don't take kindly to them."

Sabine's heart missed a beat or two, only to race at double speed afterward. Either way, she was putty in the hands of the Nazis. She smiled and projected a bravado she wasn't even close to feeling. "Well then, I'll just have to make sure I don't get caught."

"Good. You'll receive a letter with instructions tomorrow. Follow them to the T," he said.

"I will. But one more question: shall I take the bus or walk to the allotment gardens?"

The priest squinted his eyes. "How you go there doesn't

matter, but when you have the girl with you, you must take the underground. The name of the station will be in the letter."

"Thank you." Inside, Sabine rejoiced. With the name of the next station she could find the location of the allotment gardens on a city map, and then it would be as easy as counting numbers to find the correct lot.

Sabine all but danced to work and passed the day in utter excitement, blocking out all thoughts of guilt. Soon she would have Werner by her side again.

During her lunch break she walked to the payphone in the hallway and called Lily's number.

"Hello, Lily. Can we meet tonight? I have exciting news," Sabine said and for the first time since this whole spying situation had arisen, she felt like she had the upper hand.

# CHAPTER 21

After her shift, Sabine set off at a brisk pace. She arrived at the agreed-upon bench in the Tiergarten, Berlin's biggest public park, surprised to see Lily already waiting for her.

"You look very elegant," Sabine commented as she approached the other woman.

"I'm attending a formal dinner this evening." Lily lowered her voice to a conspiratorial whisper. "For work. So what's your exciting news?"

"I have finally managed to infiltrate the resistance organization. Tomorrow they'll give me instructions for retrieving and moving a Jewish girl." Sabine smiled as she finished talking, but Lily's next words deflated some of her excitement.

"A Jewish girl? That's all you came up with?" When Sabine nodded, Lily made a scoffing noise and shook her head. "Kriminalkommissar Becker isn't interested in another filthy Jewish girl. He wants the head of this organization. That's the information you're supposed to provide."

"But…"

"No buts. I'll tell you what to do. You play along with their little game and endear yourself to those traitors. Charm them. Prove your usefulness. For God's sake, if needed, even rescue that stupid girl, if it serves our goal of finding out who is in charge of organizing those activities. That's the person we need. It makes no sense to capture one girl. If we don't take down the entire organization, they will continue to smuggle Jews out of Germany."

"So, why don't we just let the Jews emigrate?" Sabine asked. "What's so bad about it? They are not welcome in our country and if they want to leave, why not let them?"

Lily pressed a hand on her chest, giving a little high-pitched gasp. "You are so naïve. Haven't you studied the work of our great Führer?"

Sabine nodded, although she wanted to say that Hitler's book *Mein Kampf*, that every couple in Germany received as a gift on their wedding day, contained pages rife with an incoherent babble of hateful notions. After not being able to derive a single meaningful thought from the book, she'd given up on reading it and had put it on the bookshelf in the sitting room where every visitor could see it.

"Jews are vermin." Lily continued her lecture, scrunching up her dainty nose as if she'd smelled a skunk. "If just one of them escapes, they will propagate like cockroaches, infesting our *Lebensraum*. No, no. Hitler says we need to eradicate them all to provide for a better world. We cannot let the seeds of a weed remain to grow and damage Germany."

Sabine objected to that analogy, and she asked herself whether Lily meant *eradicate* literally and how exactly that would be performed. But she chose not to voice her own opinion, and instead gave a noncommittal nod, saying, "Thank you for your insight. I guess I hadn't thought of things quite that way."

Lily beamed at her, basking in the knowledge she'd been able to help Sabine see the light. Sabine, though, wanted to disappear from the face of the earth. Not only was she lying to the Klausens, but also to the very people she shouldn't be if she valued her life and Werner's. Not that she liked Lily, or the Gestapo, but the constant lying, cheating and hiding nagged at her soul.

Not a single word of truth had escaped her mouth in such a long time, she worried she wouldn't remember how to be factual. Sabine had always prided herself on being an honest person, keeping her nose out of other people's business. A wave of disgust shook her shoulders as she realized what had become of her. Deceiving a priest. And a very nice one at that! Pfarrer Bernau was the kind of person who emanated peace and acceptance. In his presence Sabine had felt cosseted.

*And now you're going to betray the man... But only to save the life of another.*

Sabine gave Lily another encouraging smile and assured her, "I'll find out who's behind everything."

"Good. And I'm sure Becker will reward you. Then you can put all of this behind you." Lily put a perfectly manicured hand on Sabine's arm. "I knew you would do a good job. Call me on the telephone when you have received your instructions."

Sabine watched as Lily walked away, feeling an utter sense of hopelessness invade her soul once again. With her shoulders slumped and her eyes fixed to the ground, she returned to her temporary home.

# CHAPTER 22

S abine climbed the stairs to the apartment and reached for her key, only to freeze when she saw the door was ajar.

She gave the door a slight kick with her foot and called out, "Hello? Is someone there?"

No answer. But moments later, the door was yanked fully open and a man in a dark suit pointed his gun at her chest. "Ursula Hermann?"

A gasp escaped her throat and for lack of words she shook her head.

He seemed not to care and motioned with the barrel of his gun for her to step inside. The apartment teemed with rowdy men making quite a mess – tearing drawers from the bureau and throwing the contents to the ground, ripping open seat and couch covers, tossing crockery to the floor.

Sabine swallowed hard. *How am I going to explain this to Frau Klausen?* Although Frau Klausen was the least of her problems right now. "I'm not—"

"Sit," the man commanded, still pointing the gun at her.

"My name is—"

"Quiet! Or I shoot you! Now sit!"

Sabine snapped her mouth shut and settled onto the torn-up couch, the metal springs of its inner workings gouging painfully into her behind. She sat there, her hands shaking in her lap when several men exited the two bedrooms.

"Nothing," one of them said with a shake of his head.

*At least Frau Klausen won't notice that I searched her private room,* Sabine thought and almost scoffed at the ridiculousness of her notion. She definitely had worse problems right now. For example, the first man raising the gun at her head and saying, "Where is your hiding place?"

"Hiding place?" Sabine questioned, confused at his question.

"We have been keeping this apartment under surveillance for quite some time. You are working for the resistance..."

Sabine shook her head, "No. I really am not. This is a misunderstanding. I'm Sabine Mahler and the Gestapo ordered me—"

"We are the Gestapo and we didn't order you to do anything, at least not yet..." A cruel smile appeared on the face of the man. He apparently was in charge of the operation, because he called to another man, "Take her to the vehicle. She doesn't want to answer our questions here, so she can do so in one of our interrogation rooms."

Sabine's knees started to shake. She'd just told everything she knew to Lily, so why had Kriminalkommissar

Becker sent these men to the apartment to search it? "Look, please. I'm not the person you think…"

"That's what they all say. Do you really expect me to believe you?" the officer said.

*Probably not.* She scrambled to come up with something to satisfy him. "I gave all my information to Lily just an hour ago, and—"

"Aha…so this Lily, she's your contact person?" the officer asked.

"Yes, I'm supposed to give her all my information on a weekly basis." Sabine's voice trembled, but at least he didn't wave that gun in front of her nose anymore.

"You're coming with us. There's a lot we have to talk about," he insisted. Before Sabine could react, a burly man yanked her from the couch and out of the apartment, dragging her down the stairs. If it weren't for his brutal grip on her arm, she would have tumbled and landed in a heap of bones and limbs on the next landing.

"Where are you taking me?" Sabine asked, fear almost choking her, because she did have a pretty good idea where they were taking her. The memory of the last interrogation in the Gestapo headquarters froze the blood in her veins.

"You'll see." The man squeezed in beside her with a smug grin. "Although I doubt you'll like it."

Thirty minutes later the vehicle stopped in front of the abhorred building in Prinz-Albrecht-Strasse. Sabine did her best to remain calm and hopeful, but the violent tremble in her limbs betrayed her. Hadn't she just given Lily all the information? Shouldn't Becker be pleased instead of sending men to raid her apartment?

The Gestapo brutes manhandled her into an interrogation room similar to the one she'd been in the last time. The bare light bulb hanging down from the ceiling flickered in rhythmic intervals, giving her a headache.

Shoved into the room, she dropped onto the chair and barely managed to catch hold of the edge of the table to stabilize herself and keep from falling. "I'm not Ursula Hermann. My name is Sabine Mahler. This is a huge misunderstanding."

"Tell us the names of those you are working with," the officer demanded, ignoring her protest.

Sabine shook her head, not knowing of what they were talking. "Names? You know the names."

A fist connected with her chin. "Give us the names of the people you work with and we spare your life."

"Please…" Her lips quivered and she had to take a breath before she could voice more words. "I'm working for Kriminalkommissar Becker."

The officer dutifully noted the name and then realized what she'd said. "Liar!" The slap across her face came without a warning and Sabine pressed a hand on her burning cheek. "Tell me the truth!"

"I was ordered to infiltrate an underground network," she tried to explain.

"So you admit being a subversive?"

"No." The word came out in an exasperated yelp. "I'm not…Becker asked me to infiltrate—" Another stinging slap cut off the rest of her sentence. Sabine tasted blood in her mouth and she gingerly touched her cheek, wincing and trying not to give in to the urge to cry.

These Gestapo men didn't believe a single word of what she said. If it weren't for her dire situation, she would have laughed. One hand of the foul operation didn't know what the other one was doing.

"Tell us the names of your contact persons," the officer said, circling around her and coming to a stand behind her. "Now!" His hands came down on her shoulders and she involuntarily gagged.

"I can't. Not yet. I haven't been able to find out who else works for this organization."

"Why don't I believe you?" the officer said, hitting the back of her head. "Give me the names."

"I told you, I'm trying to get those names, but I just made contact today…"

"Lies! Nothing but lies!" the officer yelled. "Stop lying and tell me who you're working with."

"I told you already, I'm working for Kriminalkommissar Becker."

"Frau Mahler, you are skating on very thin ice. Maybe you need some time to think about your circumstances. When we return, I would suggest you be prepared to give us the names of those in the resistance organization."

He didn't have to say what the consequences would be if she failed to comply. The hard look in his eyes told her everything she needed to know. She sat on the chair after the men left, too afraid to move in case they were watching her. Her body ached from the tension in her muscles, her cheek throbbed in time with her heartbeat, and her mouth was dryer than Sahara sand.

Noises outside the door grabbed her attention and she jumped in her seat when the door suddenly opened, sure the last bells were tolling for her. But then she heard Kriminalkommissar Becker's voice saying, "This woman is working for me as an informant. I will take over her interrogation."

Relief flooded her system but turned to shock when he walked into the room flanked by two of the Gestapo brutes who'd manhandled her earlier. His hard gaze swept over her, taking in her swollen face.

"Frau Mahler, I'm sorry for the oversight of my colleagues," he said, staring at the bruises forming on her cheeks. "They can sometimes be a bit too eager to perform their duty for the Reich. Although…it's good to see you again."

Icy spiders crawled across her skin, making her hunch her shoulders. The man's lame apology didn't even come close to reaching his cold eyes.

"So tell me, what information have you been able to uncover?" He took a seat across from her, never stopping piercing her with his evil glare.

Sabine slowly shook her head, feeling her cheek throb and her hair start to come undone. One of her bobby pins had dislodged and she feared soon her hair – and her life – would come tumbling down. She blinked her eyes several times, realizing she had allowed her mind to escape. This was neither the place nor time for vanity and if she was to survive this interrogation, she had better keep her wits alert.

She took too long to answer and Becker clapped his

hands right in her face, causing her to jump in reaction. "Frau Mahler, I do not like being ignored."

"Herr…Herr Becker, I don't have any names right now… I'm supposed to move a Jewish girl and will receive instructions tomorrow. They are very careful, but I'll get more information then."

Becker shook his head, making a tsking sound. "I don't believe you. I think you are holding out on me and trying to protect those who would see the Reich destroyed. It makes me sad, very sad."

Frantic spiders scrambled all over her skin. "No, Kriminalkommissar. I would never do that. In fact I spoke with Lily Kerber just this afternoon to discuss the next steps."

Becker pursed his lips in apparent deep thought for a moment and said, "I still don't believe you. This is taking too long. I think you need a little more motivation." He nodded at the two men keeping guard on either side of the door, who slipped through the door without a word.

She took a measured breath, trying to still the nerves that were making her knees shake. A commotion in the hallway caused her to turn her head and gasp as Werner was dragged into the room by the two officers.

She barely recognized him in his torn and filthy clothing and with bare feet. His sweet face was covered with bruises, encrusted with blood, and he looked a lot thinner than when she'd last seen him.

"Werner!" Sabine surged to her feet, but before she could rush to his aid a hard grip on the shoulders slammed her back down on the chair. She turned her head slightly, and met the unyielding eyes of one of the agents who had detained her.

"Sabine? You? What?" Werner said with a weak voice only to fall silent again as one of the officers slapped him across the face, yelling, "Quiet!"

Becker nodded to the two Gestapo officers holding Werner up and they quickly handcuffed her husband on the far wall, his wrists manacled to the cuffs mounted on the cinder block wall, forcing his arms wide.

Sabine swallowed a frightened gasp when they yanked what was left of his shirt from his body, revealing the red marks on the bare skin of his back. Shaking with fear and fury she turned to Kriminalkommissar Becker, who smiled at her, seemingly enjoying the spectacle.

With her calmest possible voice she managed to say, "You promised my husband wouldn't be hurt if I did what you wanted."

"As you can see for yourself, he's still alive," the evil bastard said.

"But barely." Sabine shook her head as tears stung her eyes.

Becker shrugged. "He has proved to be a most difficult participant in our little game."

*Game? This is a game to you?* Sabine held back the angry response she wanted to give, knowing that Werner would pay for it.

One of the officers who had hauled Werner into the room produced a many-stranded whip. Becker took great joy in caressing the whip when it was handed to him, almost like he would caress a woman. He slapped it lightly against his thigh walking back and forth in the small room. "Frau Mahler, do you know what this is?"

For the life of her, Sabine couldn't utter a word, her eyes

riveted on the instrument of torture. Becker, though, didn't seem to mind. Without waiting for an answer, he continued, "This is a flogger. The Romans were especially skilled in its use and while I don't claim to be as proficient as they were...I believe I have developed a steady hand and the ability to wield it without tiring for quite some time."

He slapped it against the floor in front of her, making her jump. "Tell me what I want to know, or your husband will pay the price. Give me a name. Just one."

Sabine's eyes widened as the horror of the situation sank into her brain. She shook her head, pleading with Becker, "I've only made the first contact today, with a priest, but I don't have any other names...I need more time."

"The priest is just a messenger," Becker said, giving her a cold nod, before he walked to the far wall and brought the flogger down on Werner's back and red streaks appeared on bare skin.

"Stop! Please..." Sabine screamed drowning out Werner's pained groan.

"Tell me what I want to know," Becker demanded again.

"I don't have any names, yet. I will receive further instructions tomorrow. Please, stop hurting him," she begged, close to tears.

Becker didn't respond. He shook his hand, the flogger making swishing sounds with the movement. The next moment, Becker's face took on a very focused expression and he flogged Werner time and again.

Sabine cried out and pleaded for him to stop, while hard hands kept her firmly in the chair. She was forced to watch rivulets of blood running down Werner's back where the strands broke open the fragile skin, and she felt her heart shatter into a million pieces.

After a dozen strikes, Becker stopped. He did a slow twirl to spear her with a masterful glare, sweat beading his brow. "Are you ready to tell me what I want to know, or shall I continue?"

"Don't! I'll do anything. Anything at all, but please stop hurting my husband." Sabine didn't care that she begged. Pride couldn't live in the same universe with the Gestapo. "I don't have a name right now, but I can get you one. I promise, just give me a few more days and I'll get you the information you want. As soon as I find out where the girl is, I'll give you a telephone call. I promise."

Kriminalkommissar Becker scrutinized her for a long moment and then nodded toward the agents watching. "Very well. Cut him down and take him away."

"But...Oh, please. Don't hurt him anymore. I'll get you the information you want."

"And when you do, you shall get your husband back."

Sabine watched how the agents dragged Werner from the room. He hadn't said a word or screamed throughout the procedure, but his pained groans still filled her ears and chilled her soul. "Please don't kill him. Please..."

"Bring me the information I want and nothing will happen to your husband, but..." – an evil smirk appeared on his lips – "...don't take too long." He ordered the two agents to let her go, and disappeared.

Several minutes later, Sabine found herself standing on the sidewalk in front of the Gestapo headquarters, alone, heartbroken, terrified, and knowing that if she didn't come up with names real soon she'd be signing Werner's death warrant.

Back in the apartment, Sabine used the solitude to give in to the paralyzing fear for a moment. She sank down onto the threadbare couch, screaming her frustration into the fluffy pillow. Frau Klausen and Ursula might not be home, but the walls in this apartment had ears and eyes.

She lay on the couch, wondering how on earth she'd gotten stuck right in the middle of this mess that her life had become, when all she'd wanted to do was stay out of trouble. Forced to work as an informer for the Gestapo. Not only would she betray the Klausens, but also the kind and warm-hearted Pfarrer Bernau, and who knew how many more people.

They'd backed her into a corner, dangling the one thing they knew she loved most over her head, overwhelming her with grief and fear.

Was it wrong that she wanted to save her husband's life?

# CHAPTER 23

Sabine woke before daybreak, feeling like she'd been run over by a train. Wishing to remain hidden beneath the covers for the rest of her life, she groaned and traipsed to the front door. Since nobody else lived in the apartment at the moment, she didn't bother to put on her dressing gown or her slippers.

A piece of paper lay on the floor mocking her with its pristine white color. She slowed down her steps, approaching it carefully, as if the innocent paper would transform into a dragon and spew fire. Her heart thumping high in her throat, she waited a few moments and listened. Nothing. Not even Frau Weber seemed to be up at this ungodly hour.

Someone had braved the night to slide this piece of paper beneath her door. The instructions. Fighting the urge to return to bed and pretend she'd never existed, Sabine bent down and picked it up with her fingertips, holding it at arm's length.

With the paper unfolded, black, typewritten letters sprang at her eyes. It felt like a stroke of lightning and she let go of the paper. It sailed to the ground, flapping its wings like a bird.

Sabine left it lying and turned on her heels to attend to her morning routine first. Taking extra care with her make-up and hairdo, she dressed in her usual immaculate way. After making tea and a meager breakfast, she finally couldn't find any more reason to procrastinate and returned to the hallway to pick up the dreaded instructions.

*Pick up Ellen and take the underground from Ruhleben to Zoologischer Garten at 7 p.m. Wait beneath the big clock in the main hall with a newspaper open on page 7. Your contact will do the same.*

Sabine's breathing became quick and shallow and she had to sit down on the couch to steady her trembling knees. After a few minutes she picked up the telephone and called the number Kriminalkommissar Becker had given her.

A female voice answered, and Sabine had to wait for endless minutes until he finally took the call.

"Frau Mahler? What a pleasant surprise," his deep voice said.

*It's not pleasant at all and definitely not a surprise, you bastard.* "I...have...received my instructions. The handover will take place tonight at 7 p.m. at the station Zoologischer Garten," Sabine stammered into the receiver.

"Well done. I'm always surprised, how much a little *motivation* can boost morale." Sabine wished she could drag this depraved monster through the cord and strangle him. "You will do exactly as told, but my men will wait for you and your contact person. Don't make a foolish mistake..." The unconcealed threat in his voice reverberated through the room and Sabine swallowed hard, nodding. Then she remembered that he couldn't see her and said, "Yes."

"Good girl. Your husband will be so proud of you," Becker said and disconnected the call.

Sabine slumped against the back of the couch. As a firefighter her husband constantly put his life on the line to save others. And his wife threw others in front of the train to save him? Werner would most certainly not be proud of her.

Grateful, yes. But proud? A horrible thought entered her mind. What if he wouldn't even be grateful? What if he accused her of being a depraved monster just like *them*?

She grabbed the key for the allotment and hurried off to the factory a few minutes later, grateful for the distraction her work provided. After her shift, she went straight to the allotment area. A patchwork quilt of deep browns and vibrant greens, it consisted of vegetable patches with small huts and sheds. She stopped in front of a wooden gate with the same number as the key in her hand, taller than the height of a full-grown man, flanked by equally high thuja hedges, and opened the padlock.

Inside the hedges, the small garden glowed with vegetables and salad greens, unmistakably bearing Frau Klausen's signature. She followed the stepping stones past the water well and came to stand in front of a wooden shed. The wood showed signs of age but was amazingly well-kept. Sabine couldn't help but wonder how often the shed received guests who came to hide.

Sabine stepped inside the hut, closing the door firmly behind her, and said, "Ellen? I'm Sabine and I'm here to take you out of here and help you get to safety." It took a few moments until her eyes adapted to the darkness in the hut, lit only by sunshine filtering through cracks in the closed window shutters.

A girl crouched on the mattress in the corner and when she got up, Sabine's heart filled with compassion at the bundle of nerves in front of her. That girl was but a child and couldn't be more than twelve years old. "Come here. We need to go."

"You're not Ursula," the girl said, feeling with her hands for the wooden planks at her back.

"No, I'm not, but Ursula had to travel and sent me instead."

"How do I know you're telling the truth?" Ellen asked, her lips pursing.

"You'll have to trust me on this. We don't have time because I have to hand you over to another person in forty-five minutes." Sabine observed the emotions raging on Ellen's face and added, "I won't hurt you."

Ellen nodded and finally took a hesitant step toward Sabine. "I'm so frightened. I don't want to die."

"You won't die. Now come." Sabine extended her hand and Ellen took it. A stab of pain seared through her as she realized that Ellen's blind trust put her life in Sabine's hands...and ultimately, she'd betray her – hand the innocent girl over to the most atrocious bastards who ever roamed the earth. With Ellen's small hand lying in Sabine's they walked together to the terminus of Underground line 2 *Ruhleben*.

*How fitting*. Ruhleben meant "live in peace" and was an euphemistic name for a cemetery. It seemed like a bad omen and Sabine shuddered despite the warm May sunshine. They stepped onto the platform and waited for the train to arrive. Before the war, the trains ran every few minutes, but due to the many damaged tracks now their arrival was more hit and miss, and Sabine nervously glanced at her wristwatch.

When the train finally arrived, hundreds of people disembarked, including the conductor, who had to walk to the other side of the train to change direction. Sabine and Ellen were two of the few passengers wanting to get into the city. Everyone else had happily left it for the much safer suburbs at the end of a workday.

Eight stops until Zoologischer Garten, where she'd meet her contact person and hand over Ellen. But the Gestapo would be waiting, too. And they'd most likely take Ellen away.

Reichssportfeld. Neu-Westend. Adolph-Hitler-Platz. With every passing station, Sabine's guilt mounted, until she believed she'd suffocate from the darkness enshrouding her.

She looked at the pale young girl. Her raven-black hair hung in strands to her shoulders, the dark eyes filled with anguish – and hope. *I'm not a monster. I can't do this!* At the next stop, she jumped up, yanking Ellen's arm and said, "Hurry, we need to get off."

Ellen gave her a confused look, but fell in step behind her, barely able to keep up with Sabine's frantic pace.

# CHAPTER 24

S abine was lost, had never been in this part of the city before, and she had no idea what to do next. She continued walking, with Ellen holding her hand. Straight ahead. Not looking left or right. Walking, walking, walking. They crossed craters in the street, upended tram rails, rubble, but they didn't stop until Sabine recognized the restaurant where she'd been with Lily so many weeks ago.

At least now she had an idea how to get home from here. But the moment this thought crossed her mind, she remembered that her home didn't exist anymore. And she couldn't return to the Klausen apartment either, not with Ellen.

She'd just made a monumental decision. A watershed moment. And by choosing good over evil, she'd backed herself into a corner.

Glancing at her wristwatch she estimated that if she didn't show up with Ellen at the Zoologischer Garten within fifteen minutes, the Gestapo would know something had gone wrong. They'd kill Werner, hunt her down...

Ellen's small hand squeezed hers as if the girl had read her thoughts and looked at her with big, knowing eyes. "Something went wrong, didn't it?"

Tears threatened to spill from Sabine's eyes, but she willed them away. Not even in her lowest moment without any sliver of hope left would she let Ellen see that she was hanging on by a thread.

To sanity. To breath.

To hope.

"I'll fix it," Sabine said, not exactly sure how she'd be able to do this. But she could try. The one thing she knew was she couldn't hand over this innocent child to the Gestapo. Not even to save Werner.

She stopped, clamping her eyes shut. How could she choose between the two lives? How could she decide which life held more value? This shouldn't be happening. When had the Universe decided that she should hold the fate of two people in the palm of her hand? That she should be judge, and executioner?

Her mind raced. Werner would never forgive her for sacrificing an innocent child. After all their years together, she knew that for sure. *I'll keep Ellen safe. No matter the cost.*

But where could they go from here? The only trustworthy person who came to her mind was Pfarrer Bernau. It was a risk, but he'd know what to do. Yes, he would know.

"Come on," she said to Ellen, "we're going to see a friend for help."

They took a tram and then a bus and forty-five minutes later Sabine knocked at Pfarrer Bernau's door.

"Frau Mahler, what are you doing here with the girl?" Pfarrer Bernau hissed, his eyes wide with shock. He quickly pulled them both inside, locked the door and said, "You shouldn't have come here. What happened?"

"I'm sorry, but we needed a safe—"

He cut her off with a wave of his hand. "You're not safe with me here, and now, I'm not safe here, either. Were you followed?"

Sabine shook her head, feeling a new wave of guilt rush forward, threatening to overwhelm her again. When would it end? The horrific tornado of emotions that swirled around in her head?

"Wait here," the priest said to Sabine and disappeared with Ellen through a tiny connecting door to the church.

Sabine paced the room, waiting for Pfarrer Bernau to return, biting her lips and praying to God. Surely He would work a miracle and keep Ellen and the priest safe. When the connecting door opened again ten minutes later, she took one look at the worry on his face and broke down in tears.

"I'm so sorry. I didn't mean for this to happen."

Pfarrer Bernau wrapped an arm around her shoulders and guided her to a small bench. "Tell me what happened."

She didn't need more encouragement, and the entire story since Lily had approached her with the offer spilled forth. "Kriminalkommissar Becker promised to spare my husband's life in exchange for spying on Frau Klausen and delivering him the heads of the organization. I told him about the handover tonight, but then I couldn't do it," Sabine sobbed. "I'm such a horrible person."

Pfarrer Bernau shook his head. "War has the ability to

make saints into monsters. You did the right thing when it mattered most. Don't forget that. You saved Ellen's life today."

"But I probably killed my husband in the process and brought the Gestapo down on you and whoever else is involved."

Despite the obvious worry on his face, Pfarrer Bernau talked to her in soothing words and offered her a glass of water. While she drank he made a telephone call and shortly after, someone knocked at the door.

Sabine couldn't see the person; she only heard a female voice murmuring with the priest. From what she could glean, he tasked the woman with retrieving Ellen from the church and getting her to another safehouse.

The priest returned to his office and said, "Ellen will be safe. And you have to leave now as well."

"No! They'll be looking for me…"

"You have to go back."

"I can't. I won't," Sabine clasped her hands to the desk, as if he were physically pushing her from the room.

"It's the only way. You need to buy us some time to get Ellen out of the city and on her way to safety."

"But what do I tell them?" Sabine asked, suddenly not so sure anymore that she'd done the right thing. "I really don't want to end up in one of their torture cells."

A sad smile appeared on Pfarrer Bernau's face. "That is everyone's worst nightmare. But believe me, the more normal you act, the better your chances are. Go home. Telephone Becker and tell him that something went wrong."

"I don't think I can pull that off. I can't keep lying. Can't you see that it's killing me inside?"

"Frau Mahler, I don't see another choice. Sometimes a lie is the lesser of two evils. You saved Ellen once today, don't let it be for naught." The priest looked at her with quiet confidence and then added, "God will help you. Now go."

Sabine nodded, took a bracing breath and slipped through the connecting door into the church. She planned to find a pay phone and call Lily to tell her about the change of course. But when she passed a working telephone booth about halfway to the Klausens' apartment, she thought of a much better idea.

One that hopefully would keep both her and Werner alive for another day. She picked up her pace and took the underground to Gestapo headquarters.

# CHAPTER 25

Sabine's knees shook with terror when she stepped through the doors of Prinz-Albrecht-Strasse 8. The last two times she'd been here, she'd been in the company of Gestapo agents who'd shoved her forward.

Now, the vastness of the huge entrance hall tugged at her fear, beckoning a new wave forward. An eerie chill crept up her spine, urging her to turn on her heels and run away. She closed her eyes for a moment and took a deep breath. When she opened them again, she noticed a uniformed woman manning a reception desk.

"Good evening, I'd like to speak with Kriminalkommissar Becker, please," Sabine said, hoping her voice didn't betray her nerves.

"On what business?" the woman asked, giving her a once-over.

"He's waiting on information about some subversives. Tell him Sabine Mahler is here."

The woman reluctantly picked up the telephone and

spoke a few words. Then she pointed to a line of wooden chairs. "The Kriminalkommissar will be here in a few minutes."

"Thank you." Sabine exhaled a deep breath, sensing how a drop of sweat trickled down her temple. She brushed it away, careful not to damage her hastily renewed make-up. Becker didn't have to notice her tumbling nerves.

Becker arrived five minutes later, glaring at her. "Why weren't you at the meeting place?"

Sabine stood up. "There was a problem. I came to tell you in person. It might be important."

"Fine. Follow me," he said, leading the way deep into the maze of hallways. Sabine almost wept with joy when he stopped short of the staircase leading up to the attic with the torture cells. He opened the door to what seemed to be his office, a huge room with windows overlooking the park behind the building. It seemed to be an oasis of peace and quiet, but Sabine knew better.

The wall behind his desk was adorned with Hitler's photograph flanked by two flags with the swastika. Sabine stood for a moment and saluted the Führer. "Heil Hitler!" Her right hand shot forward, slightly above shoulder-height, the way she'd practiced it so many times in the *Bund Deutscher Mädel*, the Hitler Youth for girls.

Her salute seemed to mollify Becker, because he said with a slightly less icy voice, "Now what is so important that you came all the way here?"

"When I arrived to pick up the girl, she was gone."

"Gone?" he asked in disbelief.

"Yes. It looked like she'd been moved in a hurry." Sabine paused to let him process her words before she continued to tell her carefully rehearsed charade. "Someone warned those devious subversives. I can't think of any other explanation."

"Now you are fantasizing. Who could have done such a thing?"

"I honestly don't know. When I found out, I searched for a working telephone booth to inform Lily Kerber, just as you ordered me to." She gave him a tentative smile. "But then I had my doubts. What if she was the person who warned them?"

"Fräulein Kerber?" he scoffed. "She's not working for the resistance, I assure you."

"I can't believe it either. Lily and I attended school together and I can't possibly imagine her betraying the Reich...but she was the only one to know about the *Aktion* besides you and your men."

"Now you're implying my men are traitors?" Becker seemed to be amused at that notion.

"Of course not," Sabine hurried to say. "You and your men are above any doubt. But I thought it prudent to inform you in person, so you can investigate for yourself and find out who warned the subversives."

"Hmm..." He didn't seem convinced.

"I'm so sorry this happened. I just hope this Jewish girl won't be able to wreak havoc on Germany." Sabine dabbed at her eyes to show her immense concern.

"Who told you such nonsense?" Becker exploded. "She's a child. Vermin. How would she be able to damage our great Germany?"

Finally, Sabine felt like Becker was biting into her story. "Our Führer! He said every last Jew had the power to destroy the Master Race. And now she got away…it's my fault…I failed our Führer…" Sabine gave a sob.

"I'm sure we'll find her. Don't you worry about the vermin. What concerns me more is that we have a traitor in our own ranks," he said.

"Yes, that is very worrisome, and I can't help but wonder…who would benefit from warning the subversives? Who could be devious enough to pretend loyalty to you when in fact she's spying for them?" Sabine clasped her hand in front of her mouth. "You don't think I would do this, right? You know I'd never lie to you. I love my husband and I want him back. Besides, I wouldn't come running straight to your offices if I were the traitor. Traitors hide… they evade."

Becker gave her a long gaze and shook his head in thought. "Hmm… you have a point there. But if it's not you, then who is it?"

"It must be someone who knew about the handover." Sabine nudged him to where she wanted to have him.

"We won't jump to conclusions here, but I might have to interrogate Fräulein Kerber," he said, making a whipping movement with his hand.

Sabine felt hot and cold shivers racing across her skin. More sins piled up on her mountain of transgressions.

He pursed his lips when noticing the obvious distress on Sabine's face. "We don't take these things lightly, but since Fräulein Kerber has faithfully worked for us such a long time, I'll be gentle *if* she's really innocent."

Did the Gestapo even know the meaning of the words *gentle* and *innocent*? Sabine did her best to control her emotions and kept her voice calm when she asked, "What do you want me to do now?"

"Go home and pretend nothing is amiss. I will contact you should I need you." He dismissed her with a wave of his hand.

Sabine itched to ask questions about her husband, but she knew better than to destroy the fragile goodwill she'd just built with the Gestapo officer.

# CHAPTER 26

The May night was warm, and daylight wouldn't settle until way past ten p.m. Sabine decided to walk the long way home. She needed to think. The day had been one long succession of events. Guilt, relief, sorrow and pride fought an unrelenting battle in her confused heart.

She had done something despicable. *No. You've done a long line of reprehensible acts.* Thrown an innocent woman under the bus to save herself, although innocent wasn't exactly applicable. Lily would – and had – gladly sacrificed anyone in her way.

But knowledge of her rival's faults did nothing to lift the burden of guilt from Sabine's shoulders, and she longed to visit Pfarrer Bernau. He'd be able to set her moral compass straight, or at least he'd absolve her from her sins if she confessed. But she couldn't visit him. The Gestapo had probably followed her, and it would only serve to attract attention to her, and the priest.

No, she had to stay put. Do as Becker had ordered. Act

normal. But how did she do that when she no longer understood the meaning of the word?

Sabine took a lukewarm bath and settled onto the armchair with a cup of tea. Her entire belief system lay in tatters at her feet. How could she ever have subscribed to the opinion that minding her own business was the right course of action? Hadn't that been the most selfish way of thinking?

She fell into a troubled sleep on the couch but was awakened bright and early on Sunday morning by a loud knocking on the apartment door. She clambered to her feet, smoothing her hands over the clothing she'd fallen asleep in the night before. The knocking came again, and she hurried to open the door before it awakened the nosy neighbor, Frau Weber.

"Kriminalkommissar?" She hissed at the sight of Becker and two SS officers standing outside the door.

"May we come in?" he asked.

*So he hasn't come to arrest me.* Sabine stepped aside. "Please excuse the disarray. I was too tired to tidy up last night."

Becker stepped into the sitting room, the two SS men in their black uniforms following behind. "We captured the priest."

Sabine suppressed a shriek.

"He's still under interrogation but it seems he was the head of the organization."

"The priest?" Sabine couldn't believe her ears, sorrow about Pfarrer Bernau entering her heart. "I only met him once, but he seemed such a nice person."

Becker glared at her. "This is the very reason why the

church is a thorn in Hitler's side. Not only do her members oppose the National Socialist ideals, but also her priests are like wolves in sheep's clothing, misleading innocent citizens."

For lack of an appropriate response she nodded.

"And there's more good news," Becker said, pleased with himself. "While Fräulein Kerber hasn't confessed yet about her involvement with the resistance group, she has admitted to working for a variety of other interests, including the NKVD."

"She was working for the Russians?" Sabine's jaw fell to the floor.

"It would seem so. She had never intended to help the Reich, but only used her position for personal gain. The interloper willingly betrayed our country to the Russian secret police for a substantial amount of money."

"What's to become of her?" Despite all that Lily had done, Sabine still felt sorry for the other woman and hoped she'd at least be granted a fast and painless death.

"That is for the judge to decide, *after* we have extracted all the relevant information she possesses." The cold steel in Becker's voice chilled her to the bone and she didn't even want to consider how exactly he planned to extract that information. "But Fräulein Kerber is not your problem. Neither is Frau Klausen."

Sabine had totally forgotten about Frau Klausen and Ursula and now her stomach churned at the thought of what might happen to them. "You have arrested them, too?"

"No, they're exonerated." His lips pursed into an icy smile. "The priest confessed that he'd been tricking them into helping him by pretending that he worked under the authority of the housing agency, seeking to find new quarters for bombed-out victims."

Pfarrer Bernau had sacrificed himself to save Ursula and her mother? That man was a saint. She couldn't suppress a gasp and quickly said, "What a devious man!"

"Yes. And he'll pay the price. As we speak my men are practicing some new techniques on him." Becker's devilish smile churned Sabine's stomach. The mere sight of the odious man made her want to throw up.

She wanted to pummel her fists into his chest, pounding out every raw emotion as she demanded he let Pfarrer Bernau go free.

Observing her distress, Becker smirked and began to detail some of the torture methods used on the unfortunate souls who fell into the Gestapo's hands. She felt dizziness unsteady her and put her hand on the drawer for support.

"You look pale, Frau Mahler, are you feeling unwell?" he said, putting a hand on her arm. It took all her self-control not to yank her arm away and upset him.

"Your descriptions...this is a lot to take in on an empty stomach," she said.

"That's because you're a woman. Women are driven by emotions. They're weak, unintelligent and irrational. But..." his face came so close to hers, she could smell his breath heavy with tobacco and see the dark speckles in his irises, "...you agree that each has to be rendered his just deserts, don't you?"

She didn't think anyone should be rendered torture, but with Becker's breath brushing her face she nodded.

"Including you and your husband?"

Her eyes went wide and vomit threatened to spill into her mouth. "Me?"

"Yes." He flashed that vile smile again, torturing her with his words. An expression of gleeful delight lined his face as he basked in her terror. "You have proven a remarkably useful agent for us and I have decided to reward you for your services to the Reich by returning your husband later today."

"You will? Thank you!"

"Don't thank me. We both only followed our orders. I'll be in touch." Becker nodded at the two SS men and together they left the apartment. Sabine followed them with shaking knees, locking and bolting the door behind them.

# CHAPTER 27

Two hours later, a knock came on the apartment door. Sabine hurried toward it, wild butterflies dancing in her stomach. It was Werner! It had to be! Joy threaded through her at the expectation of seeing her husband again.

When she opened the door, she could barely suppress a gasp. Her handsome, virile husband was a mere shadow of his former self. His short brown hair had grown into a matted mess and despite his twenty-seven years, grey strands adorned his temples. His face was hollow and grey, his dirty bloodstained clothes hanging in rags from his lanky frame.

But he was alive. And free.

"Sabine," he said with a shaky voice, taking an even shakier step toward her. With great effort he made it to the sitting room and tumbled onto the couch.

"Werner, my love. You're here," she stated the obvious, showering kisses on his bruised face.

"I thought I'd never see you again after..."

"Shush. That's in the past now. You're here. Free and alive."
Sabine gingerly placed a kiss upon his lips, barely daring to
touch him for fear of causing him pain. "Are you hungry?"

"Yes. Very much so."

She drew him a bath and helped him into the tub before
she disappeared into the kitchen to prepare something to
eat. But the joy of having him back was dampened by worry
about Becker's parting shot. *I'll be in touch.* He expected her
to *continue* working for him. She'd proved remarkably
useful for the Reich. That's what he'd said.

But she wouldn't do it again. Wouldn't betray her morals
again, not even to keep Werner alive. It wasn't right.

With the potatoes boiling on the stove, she entered her
bedroom and knelt on the floor to retrieve her suitcase
from under the bed. She heaved it onto the bed and opened
it. There wasn't much inside: one single set of clothing for
Werner, including his favorite sweater. She caressed the soft
dark blue wool, remembering better times. Before all this
had happened. A queasy feeling welled up in her stomach
and for a fleeting moment she thought she'd vomit.

All the excitement of the past weeks had made her feel
unwell most of the time, but that would now change, as
soon as calm was restored in her life. She took the clothes,
except for the woolen sweater, and knocked on the bathroom door, "Werner, do you need help?"

"No, but please come in." He looked a lot better, the dirt
and blood of weeks washed away, but the bruises and cuts
still marked his flesh. Somehow he managed to smile,
showing a new tooth gap. "You can't imagine how glad I am
to be here with you."

A flush heated her cheeks. Being this near to him made her emotions bubble up, but this wasn't the moment to pursue intimacy, since she feared every touch would cause him pain. "Here are clean clothes for you. I'll be in the kitchen. Yell if you need help."

Sabine pulled the door shut and escaped into the kitchen, occupying her hands and mind with making the roast potatoes he so much loved. She found a piece of ham in the pantry and cut it into pieces to add into the pan.

Just when she finished setting the table, he suddenly stood behind her, naked from the waist up. He wrapped his arms around her waist. His embrace felt different – bony, insecure. Her heart broke when she thought about all the things the Gestapo must have done to him.

"Could you maybe have a look at my back?"

"Oh!" Tears stung at her eyes when she saw the torn flesh on his back. Red lines crisscrossed the skin, a permanent reminder of Becker's flogging. "Sit down and I'll get the first aid kit. Some of the lacerations are infected."

"No surprise."

Sabine returned with the first aid kit and carefully cleaned out the deepest of the wounds, wiping away the infection until the wound ran clear. She dabbed some antiseptic on it, wincing when Werner groaned. After placing patches across the seeping wounds, she helped him put on his shirt.

"Thank you," he said, reaching for her hand and pulling her to stand between his knees. "I love you so much…"

"I love you, too. I was so frightened they'd kill you."

"There were days when I wished they would, but then I

would close my eyes and see your face. You gave me the will to keep living."

Humbled, Sabine slid onto a chair next to him. "Eat and then you need to rest."

Werner devoured the food like a wolf and Sabine pointed toward her bedroom. "Go. I will clean up and join you."

"You are not going to work today?"

"It's Sunday."

"I didn't realize..." Werner trotted into the bedroom, where she joined him after washing the dishes and leaving the kitchen spick and span. Now that Werner was back she'd apply in the housing office for a different place to live.

She slid her shoes off and slipped onto the bed, where he was lying on his stomach. "Rest, my darling. You're safe now."

"How can you be so sure?"

"They won't be bothering us again. Not right away, at least."

Werner turned around and sat up, wincing with pain, and frowned as he looked at her face. "How do you know that? What did you do?"

Guilt came rushing back, threatening to drown her, and she stalled. "Do you know why you were arrested?"

"No. They never even told me. They simply seemed to enjoy making me scream..." His face distorted into a grimace at the memory.

A shudder racked her body and she took his hands into hers, tearing her eyes away from his gaze. But he wouldn't be fooled. They'd lived together too long for him not to know when something was wrong.

"Why do you look so guilty? Sabine, what was this all about? What did you do?"

She took a deep breath, and her voice was hoarse when she spoke, "I became their informant." Her eyes cast downward to their intertwined hands, she continued, "This apartment? You know who lives here? Frau Klausen and her daughter."

"Frau Klausen…you mean the coworker Lily wanted you to spy on?" Werner's eyes widened in shock.

"Yes. I believe it was Lily's idea to use you as leverage when I didn't agree the first time she asked me. Kriminalkommissar Becker made me an offer I couldn't refuse. Spy on Frau Klausen and bring them the head of the organization in exchange for your life."

"You agreed? You're working for the Gestapo now?" Gratitude was washed away by disgust on his face.

"It was a one-time thing, and it's not like I had a choice," she defended herself.

"There's always a choice." He pried his hands from hers.

"I chose you."

"You shouldn't have. How can I live with the knowledge that my own wife sent others into the Gestapo torture chambers just to save me? I would have preferred to die." His voice, hard as steel, slapped her, rendering her speechless. After everything she'd been through, she didn't think she could handle his rejection, too. He turned around, presenting her his back. "Go, please. I need sleep."

"Werner…"

"Go."

Sabine left the bedroom and collapsed onto the couch, only to rush into the bathroom and throw up. Her gaze fell on the mirror cabinet and another wave of revulsion hit her body.

She hadn't bled since she'd moved here, more than two months ago. Sinking onto the cold tiles, she wrapped her trembling arms around herself.

*Why now of all times?*

Several hours later Sabine was mending clothes, listening to the radio. Zarah Leander was singing *Davon geht die Welt nicht unter*, "This Isn't the End of the World". She jumped when Werner appeared in front of her and said, "We need to talk."

"About what?"

"About my wife working for the Gestapo." His face still showed disapproval over her actions.

"I'm not working for them, not anymore." She put her mending work aside and observed how he positioned himself a few steps away from her, feet hip-wide apart and arms crossed in front of his chest. She sighed, knowing he wouldn't let her off the hook until she'd told him everything. "They torched our house and assigned me to live here with Frau Klausen and her daughter."

If this revelation shocked him, he didn't let it show. "Continue."

"I was to become friendly with them..." – she remembered how that had been a failure, since Frau Klausen had suspected something – "...and when they went to visit family several days ago, I finally managed to infiltrate the resistance organization. I was supposed to move a girl into hiding."

"You handed a child over to those thugs?" Werner's eyes blazed with rage.

She shook her head, remembering the bugs in the apartment. With a finger to her lips, she stood up and turned the radio louder, before she motioned for Werner to sit with her. Since he shook his head, she went on her tiptoes and whispered into his ear, "The Gestapo can hear us."

"I don't want to sit." He glared at her.

"We'll stand then. I couldn't do it. Just before handing her over to the Gestapo, I escaped with the girl and brought her to the priest who'd arranged everything."

"You what?" His voice was hard as steel, but at least the piercing stare of his eyes had softened.

"I brought her to a safe place."

"So why did they let me go?" Werner might have been beaten to shreds, but his sharp mind still worked.

"I...I might have insinuated that someone had warned the organization."

"Someone?"

"Well, yes...I might have mentioned Lily's name." Sabine's knees trembled.

"Our neighbor, Lily? You ratted her out to the Gestapo?"

"It's not that she was innocent. It was her idea to arrest you, and she'd betrayed so many people to the Gestapo during the past years. Hundreds! She admitted it! Even if she hasn't committed this crime, her hands are steeped in blood."

He sank onto the couch, taking her with him. "You're not serious, are you?"

"Unfortunately, I am. There was no other way out. She apparently confessed to having worked for the NKVD as well. The priest sacrificed himself to clear Frau Klausen and her daughter and the Gestapo is convinced I was the one handing them the head of the organization."

"That is a lot to take in," Werner said. Silence enshrouded the room between two songs on the radio, but Sabine refused to beg for understanding. He'd have to come to his own conclusions. She wasn't exactly proud of what she'd done, but she'd been backed into a corner with no way out.

After a lengthy pause, she felt Werner's hand sneak around her shoulders. "Sabine, I'm sorry. I don't mean to sound ungrateful, but I wouldn't want you to save me at the expense of innocents. I'm glad you did the right thing when it mattered most and saved this girl. And...I guess...Lily got what she deserved."

Sabine leaned into his arms. "I'm just glad it's over."

"You know we can't stay here, right?" he said.

"I'll go to the housing agency tomorrow to ask for another housing assignment."

He chuckled into her ear. "I'm not talking about the apartment. I'm talking about Germany. We need to leave the country, or we'll never be safe."

Sabine felt the truth in his words, right down to her core. It was only a matter of time before the Gestapo would circle back and expect her to spy for them again. "You need to heal first."

"I plan on doing that quickly. Although a bit of naked care from my wife would probably be the best remedy." He cast her a wicked smile and pressed a passionate kiss on her lips.

She felt herself blush deeply as his hands slipped beneath her blouse and moved across her abdomen. Smiling at the sweet secret she carried, she decided to tell him another day. For now, she'd indulge in the love Werner wanted to shower upon her. She'd faced the devil himself and come out on the other side. Now, she'd revel in the hope, returning anew, for a better life.

The next book in the series, Trouble Brewing, will take you deep into Poland, where Richard Klausen, the missing brother of Ursula, is escaping the Soviets, rescuing a girl, being attacked by Polish partisans, and finding his strength to become a real hero.

Buy here: Trouble Brewing

Sign up to Marion's newsletter and download the short story DOWNED OVER GERMANY for free.

It tells the story of Tom Westlake, British RAF Pilot story, before he met Ursula and fell in love with her.

http://kummerow.info/newsletter-2

## ALSO BY MARION KUMMEROW

**Love and Resistance in WW2 Germany**

Unrelenting

Unyielding

Unwavering

Turning Point (Spin-off)

**War Girl Series**

Downed over Germany (Prequel)

War Girl Ursula (Book 1)

War Girl Lotte (Book 2)

War Girl Anna (Book 3)

Reluctant Informer (Book 4)

Trouble Brewing (Book 5)

Fatal Encounter (Book 6)

Uncommon Sacrifice (Book 7)

Bitter Tears (Book 8)

Secrets Revealed (Book 9)

Together at Last (Book 10)

Endless Ordeal (Book 11)

**Berlin Fractured**

From the Ashes (Book 1)

On the Brink (Book 2)

In the Skies (Book 3)

**Historical Romance**

Second Chance at First Love

Find all my books here:

http://www.kummerow.info

# CONTACT ME

I truly appreciate you taking the time to read (and enjoy) my books. And I'd be thrilled to hear from you!
If you'd like to get in touch with me you can do so via

Twitter:
http://twitter.com/MarionKummerow

Facebook:
http://www.facebook.com/AutorinKummerow

Website
http://www.kummerow.info

Made in United States
North Haven, CT
06 May 2024

52152895R00100